A bite as bad as his bark.

Although he didn't have another gun that anyone could see, Tom's hand was hurt and he still needed to fire. Sure enough, the kid went for the border shift, tossing the gun from his wounded hand into his left one. But Clint was ready for him and when the gun was in the air midway between Tom's hands, Clint reached out faster than a striking cobra and snatched the kid's pistol clean out of the air.

Tom's jaw dropped. If there weren't bullets still flying and blood still dripping onto the floorboards, the kid's expression might have even struck Clint as funny. But as it was, the furthest thing from Clint's mind was laughter.

"Think this over, kid," Clint said as he aimed one gun at him and the other at Niestrom. "I don't want to kill anyone." Even as he said that, Clint prepared himself to put a bullet through either man's skull.

After all, what a man wanted and what he had to do were oftentimes very different things . . .

D1570648

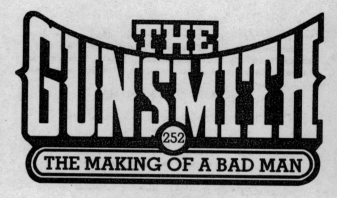

THE GUNSMITH

252

THE MAKING OF A BAD MAN

J. R. ROBERTS

JOVE BOOKS, NEW YORK

THE MAKING OF A BAD MAN

A Jove Book / published by arrangement with
the author

PRINTING HISTORY
Jove edition / December 2002

Visit our website at
www.penguinputnam.com

ISBN: 0-515-13420-1

A JOVE BOOK®
Jove Books are published by The Berkley Publishing Group,
a division of Penguin Putnam Inc.,
375 Hudson Street, New York, New York 10014.
JOVE and the "J" design
are trademarks belonging to Penguin Putnam Inc.

PRINTED IN THE UNITED STATES OF AMERICA

10 9 8 7 6 5 4 3 2 1

ONE

"Oh my," the young lady said while reaching out with a tentative hand. "Can I touch it?"

The only light in the room came from the warm, dusky rays of the setting sun. Most of the beams were kept out by a set of curtains drawn across the window, but those that made it through gave the walls a rich, soft texture, which took the edge off the slight chill in the air. Even though her face was mostly obscured by a filmy shadow, the excited glint in her wide eyes could be seen as clearly as a new day.

Sitting across from her was a kid in his late teens, wearing the smirk of a cat who'd just managed to trap a mouse by its tail. "You want to touch it?" he asked with exaggerated caution. "I don't know if you should. It might not be proper."

The girl was about his age, give or take a year, and sat Indian-style on the end of a small rectangular bed. Her black hair came down just past the nape of her neck and curled at the ends in a way that framed her face and made her light-colored skin seem even softer than it actually was. All of her clothes except for the bare essentials were lying on the floor next to the bed, leaving her in nothing

1

but a flimsy white camisole and a cotton skirt which wasn't much more than the bottom half of a slip. The longer she stared down at him, the more her nipples became visible through the thin layer of material.

"It's so big," she said. "I want to hold it." Full, red lips curved in a wicked little smile, and when she moved her creamy brown eyes up to meet his, they betrayed a little more experience than the almost childlike quality of her voice.

The kid didn't catch that part, however. He puffed out his chest and flashed his most winning smile, which, despite its youth, still held an undeniable charm. "You want to hold it, darlin'? Then you go right ahead."

With that, he leaned his back against the headboard, spread his legs, and straightened his right arm toward her. Clutched in his hand was a Smith and Wesson .44 revolver that was so new it shone without having to be polished once. Just as the girl was about to take the gun from him, he spun it in his hand and pulled it away. When the gun came to a stop, it was pointing at the girl's heart, its hammer snapping back with a well-oiled *click*.

The glint in her eyes became even brighter and her breath caught in the back of her throat. "Oh," she purred while wriggling her upper body slightly. "That was so fast."

"I know. Plenty of men out there died with that sight bein' the last thing on their minds. But you, darlin', get to live to tell the tale."

Thomas Bolander held the gun out once again and this time he let her take it from him. He savored the way she tentatively slid her fingers along the pearl barrel and stroked it all the way down to his fingers. She didn't take it by the handle, but instead let the weapon rest in the palms of her hands as though it was an offering. Her thumbs moved back and forth over the gleaming steel.

Tom's dusty brown hair stuck out like a poorly tended

shrub sprouting from his scalp. Having always had his father cut it with a razor whenever it got too unruly, Tom looked much the same now as he did when he was a sprout himself. The clear blue eyes and occasional attempt at chin whiskers made him look even more boyish, although he would have denied that fact to the death.

Watching the girl in front of him handle his gun made Tom's thoughts wander and his mouth turn dry. He couldn't stop following her fingers with his eyes, studying the way she gently stroked the pistol. When she looked up at him again, Tom snapped his eyes back to hers and forced a cooler look onto his face.

"Have you killed anyone with this?" she asked.

There was a silent moment that seemed to crawl by on turtle's legs. The girl knew she was being watched and had an even better idea of the effect she was having on the young man. She wasn't stupid, after all, since she made a good amount of her living by getting herself into situations very much like this one. Her name was Abby Tyler and though she was only one year older than Tom, the experience she'd acquired in that time was enough to make her feel ten years his senior.

None of that experience came off as weariness, however. Much the contrary, it gave her an exotic look about her, which came through from the way she smiled right down to the slinky, catlike movements of her body. It was no mistake that she wrapped her hand around the gun and held it while her eyes happened to drop down to the growing bulge in Tom's pants. But the flush in her cheeks was genuine as she stared at him intently and the chill that ran beneath her skin was impossible to fake.

Finally, Tom was able to figure out an answer to the question he'd been asked. "Yeah. Of course I have. Plenty of men." Unfortunately, that was the best he could come up with at the moment.

Abby wasn't sure if she believed him or not. Even

though her first instinct was to take everything the kid said with a grain of salt, she weighed that against the other things she knew about him. Highest on that list was who Tom rode with.

For the moment, Abby decided to not trouble herself with what she thought. More pressing right then was what she felt. And the longer she held that gun and allowed herself to drift closer to Tom, the more intensity she could feel coming off of him. Like kerosene on a fire, that intensity made her own cravings blaze that much brighter and soon she was closing her eyes and tilting her head invitingly.

Tom might not have been familiar with all female subtleties, but he didn't have to be hit over the head with one either. The moment he saw that Abby looked like she wanted to be kissed, he was right there to oblige. Their lips met softly at first, increasing in intensity the first time Abby let the tip of her tongue brush against his lip.

When they finally broke apart, Abby was flushed with excitement and she gripped the pistol tight enough to whiten her knuckles. Without breaking eye contact, Tom reached out and took the .44 away from her and slid it back into its holster.

Abby crawled forward on the bed with slow, sinewy movements. The top of her camisole hung down to expose the tops of her breasts as they swung back and forth with her approach. The nipples were small, pink and erect, brushing against the material in a way that stoked the fires inside of her even more.

Although Tom started to get up, his movement was stopped by Abby's hand placed flat against his chest. Curling the tips of her fingers, she scratched him just hard enough to get his attention before pushing him back down against the headboard.

"You don't have to move another inch," she whispered. "I want to take care of you now."

Tom didn't even begin to protest. Wearing a grin that was almost wide enough to consume his entire face, he dropped his shoulders against the headboard and let Abby straddle his hips. There was a moment of concern when he felt her fingers hook beneath his gun belt and start working the buckle, but once she'd pulled the two halves apart, she peeled it away from his body and laid it across his chest.

"Mmmm, I like that gun of yours," she said softly.

Tom's right hand went automatically to the pistol. "Is that a fact?"

Straightening up and arching her back, Abby ran her hands between his legs. The flimsy camisole clung to her breasts like a second skin. "Not that one," she said while sliding her fingers between Tom's legs. "This one."

Smiling, Tom set the gun belt on the floor next to the bed.

TWO

The Yellow Dog Saloon wasn't exactly the most attractive part of the small town of Clark, West Virginia, but it was certainly one of the most popular. Sporting a pair of bars and an owner who mixed up his own whiskey in a still out back, the saloon catered to anyone willing to pay their bill. Its claim to fame, besides the mangy mutt which was hardly ever away from its spot in the back corner, was the neutrality of its patrons.

Everyone from the law to the lawless came to the Yellow Dog and it was accepted as fact that none of their problems with one another followed them inside. That wasn't to say that the place was overly peaceful. It was just somewhere akin to holy ground.

No fights started there, although plenty of them came to a head in the street outside its door. That, along with the whiskey, the mixed company and the old dog sleeping in the corner was what made the saloon a required stop for anyone in the know when they were in town.

There was always someone worth talking to at the Yellow Dog. At least, that's what the rumors said. And if a man got there when it was quiet, all he had to do was

6

wait and someone fitting the bill would walk through the door.

Someone like John "Third Eye" Niestrom. A lanky man with dark red hair and pale skin, Niestrom had scars on his face that were just as deep as the dimple in his chin, all of which gave him the kind of natural character that inspired strong emotion the first time he met someone new.

Folks either loved or hated him. Usually, the choice between those two was made by Niestrom himself who was an expert at handling people with just as much skill as he handled his custom-made guns. He didn't have to talk much or even initiate any conversation. All he had to do was fix a target with his eyes in a certain way and he would be halfway down the road to putting forth whatever image he felt like projecting that day. It was all in the eyes. That's what he said and that's what he believed.

Of course, having one eye that was gray as gunmetal and another that was milky white, Niestrom had an edge over most people when it came to using their eyes to create an impression.

His reputation as a gunfighter was especially widespread farther south, but he was fairly well known in these parts as well. In the Yellow Dog, however, he was the next best thing to legend.

"What can I get for ya, Mister Niestrom?" the gray-haired barkeep asked as he placed both hands flat on top of the bar in front of the smaller man.

"How about a beer?" the gunfighter replied.

"Not another one of my whiskeys? I made this batch fresh this mornin'."

Niestrom shook his head and waved away the offer as though it was a lazy fly circling his head. "Not just yet, thanks. I need to stay sharp for a while yet. Any more of that concoction of yours and I'm likely to be spending the rest of the night stretched out on this here floor."

"All right, then. But if I don't serve you some whiskey while you're in town, I'm likely to get offended."

"We can't have that, now can we?"

"Absolutely not." The barkeep filled a fresh mug from the keg to his right and set the beer in front of Niestrom. "Glad to see you back in Clark. How long you plannin' on staying?"

Niestrom took a healthy swig of the bitter brew before answering. "Hell if I know. Guess I'll leave that up to my partner."

"Partner? Last I heard, you always rode alone."

If that came from anyone else but the Yellow Dog's barkeep, Niestrom might have been suspicious or maybe even a little cross at having someone question his comings and goings. But Dave was known for keeping up with his patrons, even if they only came through once or twice a year. In fact, if Dave *hadn't* known a thing or two about Niestrom, the gunfighter might have felt like he'd been dropped down a notch or two in the pecking order.

"Sharp as ever, Dave," Niestrom said while tipping his mug in salute. "But you must not've heard the latest."

The barkeep's face became intent and he leaned forward to rest his elbows upon the polished wooden surface. "Really? Then how about filling me in?"

"I'm riding with a kid by the name of Tom Bolander."

"Taking him under your wing?"

Niestrom chuckled once and shrugged. "Nearly put a bullet in the little cuss when I first met up with him in Iowa, but I admired the kid's pluck. That, and the fact that he covered my ass when I was blasting my way out of a bank robbery two days later convinced me he might be worth my time."

One of the other men in the bar turned around when he heard that. A tin star on his chest caught some of the light drifting in through the front window, and played across his narrowed eyes. The lawman was obviously interested in what the gunfighter was saying, but he didn't budge from his seat. Instead, he went back to his drink and shook his head subtly to the deputy sitting across from him.

Whoever the lawman was, he would store the bit of conversation away for later. This was what brought folks to the Yellow Dog and starting any trouble now would simply dry up this invaluable resource for collecting information and juicy bits of gossip.

It was hard to say whether Niestrom didn't notice the lawman sitting at the other table or if he just didn't care. He shifted his weight from one foot to another and went on with his story. "He's not bad for a kid that's still wet behind the ears. Hell, he even reminds me of me when I was his age . . . however long ago that was."

Both men chuckled at the joke and Dave straightened up so that he was no longer leaning into the conversation. "So where is this kid? I'd like to meet him."

The sound that came out of Niestrom's throat was a rough cross between a groan and a snarl. "Last I saw of him, he was sweet talkin' some dark-haired girl. He took off with her a while ago and I ain't seen him since."

"Ahh," Dave said knowingly. "You mean Abby. She comes here quite a bit. Likes to soak up the atmosphere if I'm not mistaken. If your friend left with her, he might be busy for a little while. She tends to favor the rougher kind." Suddenly, Dave stopped short and he winced slightly. "Hope I didn't offend you, John."

"Hell, I been called a lot worse than that. Why don't you set me up with one of them whiskeys. I thought Tommy might be getting his tadpole wet, but now that I know for sure, I might as well settle in."

Smiling, Dave said, "Here, here," while bending down to take a glass from beneath the bar. He tossed the glass from one hand to another in a well-practiced move and walked toward a row of bottles lined up on a shelf on the wall. None of the bottles were labeled and every one of them was filled with a murky brown liquid that seemed to catch the light and swirl it around like bits of leaves in pond water.

"You may be stuck here for a while," Dave said after filling Niestrom's glass. "But you might as well make the most of it."

"What're you talking about?"

Leaning in once again in his familiar way, Dave set his chin on the back of one hand while hooking his other thumb toward the opposite end of the bar. "See that fella standing over there?"

Niestrom glanced in that direction and immediately spotted a tall, lean figure nursing a beer. "Yeah. What about him?"

"That's Clint Adams. He breezed in here just before you got here and has been holding court with nearly every other soul in this place."

"He taking any challenges, or just doing a bad job of keeping a low profile?"

"Neither," Dave replied with a shake of his head. "Just seems to know a lot of folks and doesn't mind talking to them. I could introduce you if you'd like."

Niestrom took a closer look at the other man Dave was talking about. The first thing that ran through his mind was that the quiet, unassuming figure couldn't possibly be Clint Adams. How could he be standing in the same room as the Gunsmith and not even know about it? But then again, if that was going to happen in any place in this part of the country, it would happen in the Yellow Dog Saloon.

Niestrom thought about what he knew concerning Clint Adams. Besides the normal things, which ran the gamut from rumor to myth, he realized he didn't know a whole lot. There were plenty of folks who said the same thing after meeting up with him.

Adams was supposed to be a stand-up man who was fast with the iron.

Not just fast. *Real* fast.

"I think I'll take you up on that introduction," Niestrom said with a murderous glint in his eye. "I'd like that very much indeed."

THREE

Saloons like the Yellow Dog were nothing new to Clint Adams. Usually any place big enough to be considered a town rather than a village or camp had a watering hole with some degree of notoriety. Whether or not that notoriety was real or the creation of the saloon's owner was never much of an issue.

All that mattered was that the liquor was good and that it never ran out. That, along with things like gambling and women were normally enough to keep most places in customers for a while. Everything else was just atmosphere.

Clint had been to plenty of saloons that boasted some degree of fame. Such places were nothing new to him in the least. In fact, they were easier to come by than a good steak. But the Yellow Dog wasn't just any watering hole. There was something about that place that drew people to it like ants to a picnic. And no matter how many other saloons Clint had ever been to, even he had to admit that there was only one Yellow Dog.

Even the roughest killers treated the place with a certain amount of reverence. Nobody really knew where that

came from or why it started, but it was there all the same
and nobody really seemed to mind.

Clint had been passing through the area when he realized that Eclipse would be taking him within a few miles
of Clark, West Virginia. And the next thing in his mind
after that was the Yellow Dog Saloon. All of the lawmen
he'd ever talked to about that place said they liked it because of all the good information they could soak up just
by sitting in one of Dave's chairs for an hour or two.
Plenty of unsavory types had met their end after flapping
their gums too long at the Yellow Dog.

As for some of the less reputable characters Clint had
shared a drink with, every one of them had a kind word
to say about the Yellow Dog. That saloon was a place to
go to catch up with old friends and keep track of their
worst enemies. Outlaws got more news there than from
any of the country's best newspapers. More than that, they
felt they could truly relax there. When they walked out
of the Yellow Dog and into the regular world again . . .
that was another story.

Clint liked the Yellow Dog because it was a place for
him to go where it didn't matter who he was. After keeping his eyes open and watching his step every minute of
every day, it was nice to head someplace that didn't carry
the threat of a fight. Even if it was just within the Yellow
Dog's walls, such easy times were worth their weight in
gold.

Besides, Clint never really knew who he might find
when he walked into that particular saloon. It could be an
old friend whom he'd lost track of over the years. It could
be someone he might've met over a game of cards two
weeks ago. At the moment, it didn't matter much to Clint
because he knew there would be someone.

Much to his surprise, that someone turned out to be
quite a few someones who'd been passing through on
their way to a poker tournament in Wheeling. Since his

arrival at just past noon that day, Clint had met up with no fewer than a dozen or so friendly faces.

He'd been drinking a steady supply of beer, none of which he'd had to pay for. The hours had flown by over conversations, swapping stories and even trading raunchy jokes before the old Friends Clint had met up with had had to find their way out the door.

For the moment, Clint was by himself and mulling over everything that had gone on since his arrival into town. It wasn't anything earth shattering, but it was enough to make Clint's slight detour completely worthwhile. In fact, this was exactly why he'd decided to come to the Yellow Dog in the first place.

Clint swirled the last of his beer around the bottom of his mug, wondering what he should order for dinner. Although it had felt good to be on his feet after coming in off the trail, his legs were starting to cramp up and it was about time for him to find a nice chair in front of an even nicer meal. Unfortunately, the Yellow Dog was not well known for the skill of its cook.

It took Clint less than a couple of seconds to think back to the last time he was in town and soon after that, he recalled the place where he'd had a good hot meal. If memory served him correct, the place was no more than a block or two down the street and was more than worth the short walk.

Pouring the last bit of beer into his mouth, Clint took a step away from the bar and turned toward the door. His way was immediately blocked by a man who was skinny as a rail and seemed to be made from the same kind of material.

"You Clint Adams?" the man asked.

Before Clint could answer, he saw the barkeep dashing his way.

"This here is John Niestrom," Dave said by way of introduction. "I told him you were here and he wanted to meet you. I hope you don't mind."

FOUR

"No," Clint said evenly. "I don't mind a bit." He glanced over the skinny man with a quick, practiced eye. He knew better than to judge the other man on physical stature alone since that didn't account for much in the grander scheme of things.

Some of the deadliest men weren't much to look at. Thinking along those lines, Clint was reminded instantly of Doc Holliday. There was a sickly, pale Georgian who could walk out of a storm of bullets and toss back a case of whiskey while winning a fortune at cards. Although he doubted this man was in Doc's league, Clint kept himself from drawing any conclusions for the moment.

"Nice to meet you," Clint said while offering his hand. "Have we met somewhere before?"

"No," Niestrom replied. "If we had, you would've remembered it, that's for damn sure."

Clint recognized the look in Niestrom's eyes. He'd seen it plenty of times in plenty of places. It was the intense, hungry look of a predator sizing up his prey. Instinctively, Clint looked down at Niestrom's hands, making sure they weren't drifting toward his gun.

The gunfighter seemed anxious enough, but he wasn't

15

stupid. His arms were steady as rocks and far enough away from his holster to put Clint somewhat at ease.

"I was just about to leave," Clint said in a voice meant to test the man in front of him. "So if you don't mind, I'd like to be on my way."

Dave seemed completely oblivious to what was going on just beneath the surface between Clint and Niestrom. "Headed out of town so soon, Mister Adams? That's a shame."

"Not out of town. Just out to get a bite to eat. That is unless that poses a problem for anyone." When he said that last sentence, Clint looked pointedly down at Niestrom. Even though the gunfighter only stood an inch or two shorter than him, Clint managed to make it seem as though he was glaring down at a misbehaving child.

Niestrom bristled at the look in Clint's eyes, but couldn't deny the power in his stare. In response, Niestrom didn't say a word. Instead, he held back a scowl and felt the chill, which normally came just before he removed another soul from this world sweep through his bones.

"I don't mind at all, Mister Adams," Dave said good naturedly. "Just be sure to come back soon. There's been plenty of folks askin' about you and they'd be happy to hear you're in town."

Keeping his eyes fixed on Niestrom for another second, Clint waited until the smaller man looked away before glancing toward the barkeep. "I just need to get some food in my belly, Dave. I'll be back as soon as I'm done. Are there any good card games in town?"

"Clark's been off the gambler's circuit for a while now, but there's always someone looking to play. If you'd like, I'll put the word out myself. I'm sure I'll get some takers."

Clint nodded once to the barkeep. He knew that he didn't have to worry about Dave advertising the fact that he was in town just to fill some more seats in his saloon.

The only thing Clint had to worry about was dealing with high-caliber card sharps who were drawn to the Yellow Dog just as he'd been. But of course, that was half the fun of playing poker.

"Thanks, Dave," Clint said. "I'll see you in awhile."

Niestrom waited for Clint to start walking before taking a quick sidestep, which placed him directly in the other man's path. "Mind if I sit in?"

When Clint turned to look at the gunfighter, he moved slowly enough to make Niestrom wait. "Only if you don't mind losing." The heat in his eyes was nearly enough to steam the paper off the walls. And when he started walking again, Clint noticed that he didn't have to ask for Niestrom to get out of his way.

What might have been a dangerous moment passed quickly into the saloon's background noise. Clint walked out of the Yellow Dog without looking back, and Niestrom let him go without bothering him. Any other place at any other time, and the gunfighter would have felt it was his duty to repay such a comment no matter whose mouth it came from.

But this wasn't just any place. It was the Yellow Dog and there were certain things a man just didn't do on sacred ground.

After the saloon's front door swung shut and slapped loudly against the frame, Niestrom shook his head and laughed in spite of himself. He had a healthy respect for Dave's place, but he had no idea that his respect ran so deep. He couldn't exactly say why or what had caused it, but Niestrom just felt like he was under a certain set of rules when he was in these walls.

Those rules didn't apply to the rest of the world, however. And since Adams wasn't the type to run away, Niestrom figured he'd get another shot at the Gunsmith later on that evening.

"You all right, John?" Dave asked as he made his way

over to where Niestrom was standing. "You look like you're about to burst."

In the time it took for Niestrom to turn and look at the barkeep face-to-face, the smile he was wearing lightened up a bit and started to seem at least partially genuine. "Nah, I'm all right."

"Hope you didn't have any cross words with Mister Adams. In case you don't know, he's—"

"I know who he is," Niestrom interrupted. "Just do me a favor and make sure to save me a spot in that card game you're setting up. Think you can do that?"

Dave nodded without a moment's hesitation. "Sure, John, sure." With a wink, he added, "Maybe I should take a fee for reserving seats in a game like that one, huh?"

Niestrom shot the bartender a look that could have melted the glass right out of the Yellow Dog's windows.

"Not from you, of course," Dave said as he shrank away from the gunfighter's stare. "I'm just saying that there's plenty of men who'd be willing to pay for a seat at that table. You stand to make some good money. I know for a fact that Adams doesn't mind playing for high stakes."

"I've heard that same thing. And if I have anything to say about it, the stakes tonight are going to be high enough to make even a Gunsmith sweat in his boots." Niestrom settled back into his place at the bar. "Where the hell is that kid?"

FIVE

Tom sat on the bed facing Abby, moving only when it was absolutely necessary as he let the young woman peel the clothes from his body. He relished the feel of her hands as they worked over his skin, savoring every moment that brought him closer to being able to get his hands on her smoothly contoured figure.

At first glance, Abby looked like a small girl. The dresses she wore did a good job of hiding the sumptuous curves of her large, full breasts and the hourglass shape of her hips and waist. When she'd finally managed to pull Tom's pants off over his feet, she stayed at that end of the bed and straightened up on her knees.

She locked her eyes with his and let her hands wander down over her skin. Allowing her fingertips to catch in the top of her blouse, Abby pulled the fabric down just enough to expose one breast. Once there, she closed her eyes and touched herself in the exact spots that she liked the most, guiding Tom by her own example while pleasuring herself at the same time.

Watching this, Tom felt his own passion stirring deep within him. He couldn't take his eyes away from Abby as she rolled her erect nipple between thumb and forefinger while letting out a slow, passionate moan. He was almost hesitant to reach out to her, just in case doing so might cause her to stop what she was doing.

So rather than try to take over, he slid his hands up and down along her legs. Abby's skin was smooth and moist with perspiration. It wasn't that the room was especially warm, but the heat being generated from their proximity was enough to bring about the little beads of moisture, that glistened on her flesh and caused her undergarments to stick to her body.

Temporarily lost in her own world, Abby's head dropped back as she all but tore the camisole off and clasped both hands to her breasts. Feeling her touch upon her sensitive skin while knowing that Tom was right there watching her caused her to become even more excited than she already was. When her eyes opened again, they were alight with an intense fire.

The first thing she noticed was Tom's hands making their way up to her hips. Abby scooted forward on top of him and reached down to cover his hands with hers. Purring quietly under her breath, she guided his hands along her body and between her legs until his fingers were brushing over her swollen clitoris.

"That's it," she whispered. "Right there. Don't stop."

This wasn't Tom's first time in a woman's bed, but this was one of the only times he'd gotten such exclusive attention from one. Normally, they just allowed him to satisfy himself while doing whatever they could to speed him along his way. Now, he was being guided and instructed by Abby in a way that made him never want to leave that room. More than that, he never wanted his hands to leave her skin.

Tom's penis was rigid and aching to be inside of her. The more he explored Abby's body, the more he wanted to throw her down and climb on top of her. The only thing that made him feel better than touching her was the sweet torture of denying himself what he wanted more than anything else in the world at that moment.

Sensing this, Abby smiled and looked at him through smoldering eyes. "You want to be inside of me?"

Tom's answer to that was given through his hands rather than his voice. Still rubbing gentle circles on and around her vagina, he placed the tip of one finger just inside the lips between her legs and slid it slowly inside. Her entire body reacted to the penetration and every one of her muscles tensed.

Breathing in deeply, Abby leaned back and spread her legs open a little more. "That's good."

Leaning forward, Tom slipped another finger inside of her and pushed it in all the way.

"Oh, god," Abby moaned. "That's so good."

Tom couldn't take his eyes off of her as she arched her back and let herself become completely engrossed in the moment. He didn't even notice her hand reaching out for him until her fingers closed around his penis and started stroking in time to his thrusting fingers.

Now it was Tom's turn to lose track of the world around him as waves of pleasure started pulsing through his entire body. Those seconds seemed to last all night long, both of them facing each other and stoking their fires until one of them cracked under the pressure.

It almost came as a surprise that Abby was the first one to break contact. She pulled her hands away and took hold of Tom by the wrists. Smiling seductively, she moved his hands up to her mouth and kissed them gently, sucking on his fingers while teasing them with her tongue.

Unable to wait any longer, she moved up even closer to him until she was positioned in his lap. Abby wrapped both legs around Tom's waist and pulled herself even tighter, guiding the tip of his cock between her legs with one hand.

Tom reached around behind the girl and cupped her

bottom with both hands. Her buttocks were round and finely contoured and she squealed with delight when she felt herself being pulled in against him and his body pumping easily into hers.

Their bodies quickly found a rhythm; Abby bouncing up and down on top of Tom while he thrust his hips back and forth. After all the anticipation leading up to this moment, the sensations were intense enough to send hot flashes beneath their skin.

Abby moved with strength and precision, allowing Tom to guide her, yet twisting every once in awhile in a way that he would never have though of. Once she'd managed to position herself so that he was rubbing her in just the right way, Abby held on to him with every bit of strength she could muster and let him pound into her with all his youthful vigor.

As their bodies writhed on top of the bed, Tom enjoyed the feeling of Abby's muscles moving under his hands. She strained with the effort of their lovemaking with such passion that it made Tom want to satisfy her even more.

But his entire mind wasn't focused on that. She was making him feel as though there was lightning running throughout his entire body. Every time he pushed into her, Abby's body closed in around him, squeezing him in an intimate massage, which brought groans of pleasure from both of them as he pulled out again.

When she felt her climax approaching, Abby placed both hands on Tom's shoulders and leaned back while digging her nails into his skin. Tom soaked in the gorgeous view of her breasts and heaving stomach as his own orgasm began to pump the blood even faster through his veins.

Abby started to scream, but stopped herself by biting down on her lower lip. Tom didn't need to go through such restraint because his own pleasure was so intense that it robbed him of all his breath for a good couple of seconds.

In fact, those were some of the best couple of seconds in all his eighteen years.

Their energy depleted, both of them nearly collapsed on top of each other. Tom was able to ease himself down onto the bed and Abby settled in on top of him. She wriggled a bit to get herself comfortable and managed to keep him inside of her.

"Good lord," Tom said once he caught his breath. "That damn near killed me."

Abby accepted the compliment with a smile and traced looping designs on his shoulder. "You know, I heard you were good with that gun of yours, but I had no idea."

SIX

The only thing Clint remembered about the restaurant he favored in Clark was a vague set of directions. The last time he'd been in town, he recalled coming out of the Yellow Dog, taking a . . . left and then turning at . . .

His mind fought to get a better grasp on that elusive bit of information as he stood outside of the Yellow Dog looking like he'd forgotten his own name. Just as Clint was about to throw up his hands and march into the nearest store for directions, the clog in his memory let loose and everything he'd been looking for suddenly came back to him.

Not only could he remember where the restaurant was, but he could even recall what he'd had the last time he'd been there. The steak and potatoes were pretty good, but it was the freshly baked cherry pie that truly stood out. Clint's mouth watered the more he thought about it. With the directions firmly in mind, his feet took him where he wanted to go, allowing Clint to enjoy the cool air and the quickly darkening sky.

The restaurant was called Mil's Place. It stood at the end of Third Avenue sandwiched between a general store and one of the few saloons in town that dared to compete with the Yellow Dog for business. Despite the reputation of its competition, that saloon seemed to be doing all right for itself and there was a steady flow of bodies moving through the flapping batwing doors.

As for Mil's, the restaurant was just the way Clint remembered it: quiet, small, warm and full of the smells of fresh cooking. Clint walked inside and took the place in, nodding to himself with the knowledge that his memory wasn't as bad as he was starting to fear. Even the tables were arranged in a familiar way, making it a course of habit for Clint to walk over and sit at what might very well have been the same spot he'd occupied last time.

"Be right with you," came a woman's voice from the back of the room. "Get ya something to drink?"

Clint found a menu folded in half and wedged between a salt and pepper shaker. "Sure," he said while retrieving the list of selections. "How about some cold tea?"

"Coming right up."

Even though his eyes scanned up and down the handwritten menu, Clint was merely going through the motions. The vivid memories of his last meal there were too strong for him to want anything but a repeat performance. His heart jumped a bit for a moment, but then he spotted what he wanted on the back of the menu right above the list of desserts. He took it as a good sign that peach pie was at the top of the list.

Clint looked up just in time to see the door to the kitchen fly open and a plump blond woman hurry through carrying a tray that looked as though it weighed more than she did. She bore the weight with a harried grin and tossed Clint a friendly nod.

"Your tea's right here, mister," she said. "I just need to drop off these folks' dinners."

Clint smiled back at her. "No hurry. I'm too hungry to run away on you."

The waitress held Clint's eye for another moment before turning her full attention to the table that was her destination. With a bit of friendly banter, she set plates down in front of the family of four seated there and cleared away some of their empty bread plates. Finally, once those customers were squared away, she hurried over to Clint and placed a tall glass of tea in front of him.

"There you go," she said. "Sorry to keep ya waiting. What can I get for you?"

"Well, you can do me a favor and take a seat here." Grinning, Clint kicked out the chair to his right.

"Much as I'd like to, I'm in the middle of working and I couldn't—"

"Not for a whole meal or anything. Just take a moment to catch your breath before you pass out." When Clint saw that she still wasn't too receptive to the notion, he tilted his head and stared her right in the eyes. "Come on, I insist. Besides, isn't the customer always right?"

Although she still didn't seem completely at ease, the waitress set her tray down on the table and moved over to the chair Clint had indicated. Every trace of her resistance faded the moment she put her weight on that chair. She even seemed a little embarrassed by the relieved sigh that escaped from her mouth.

"Lord above, that does feel good," she said while stretching her feet out beneath the table. "Bless your heart."

Clint smiled at the attractive blonde and took a sip of his tea. "I know what it's like to spend a lot of time on your feet. And it does me some good to see you smile like that."

The waitress set her order pad on the table and leaned toward Clint. "I'd better see what you want before I get too comfortable. If that happens, you might have a hard time getting rid of me."

"That doesn't sound like too hard of a time to me."

Despite the edge in the waitress's voice that had been

sharpened after having every other male customer that came into Mil's flirt with her, she softened just a bit when she looked into Clint's eyes. "Why don't you start off with giving me your order. After that . . . we'll see."

"Good enough. My name's Clint."

"Sandra."

"I'm in the mood for a steak. Are they as good as I remember?"

"Probably better. We got a new cook just last week and he puts the last one to shame."

"Even better."

"Since you gave me this little rest, I'll even wrangle you a piece of pie for free. Be sure to save some room."

Clint winked. "There's always room for pie."

Sandra shook her head and groaned at that as she got back to her feet. The smile stayed in place on her lips, however, which was all Clint had been shooting for.

SEVEN

Tom felt like he was still in a daze when he opened the door to Abby's room and stumbled outside. He was hitching up his pants as he made his way down the hall, buckling his belt right before he attempted to climb down the stairs.

Behind him, Abby stood and watched him go, a wicked little smirk playing on her lips. She waited for him to stop and turn around, knowing that he would, and blew him a kiss when he finally obliged. Although he was somewhat reluctant, Tom acknowledged the kiss with a parting wave and descended to the floor below.

As soon as he got out into the world again, Tom felt his chest start to swell with pride and his steps to take on some additional steam. The people he passed looked at him with a mixture of respect and envy. At least, that was how Tom read their faces as he strode past them on his way out the front door.

The hotel was down the street from the saloon that Niestrom had been so fixed on going to, which made it all the more surprising that he'd been able to get out from the older man's watchful eye. Niestrom had taken it upon himself to watch Tom like a hawk.

Actually, Tom had to remind himself that that wasn't exactly the truth. When he'd first met up with the gunfighter, Tom wanted nothing more than to learn from Niestrom and hone his own natural talent with a gun. The day that Niestrom agreed to their current arrangement had been one of the most rewarding in Tom's life and every day since then had been an eye-opening experience.

Tom had learned more from John Niestrom than he had from any of his school teachers. He'd come farther than he'd ever thought possible, which was saying a lot since Tom's father had raised him to believe that he would never leave his farm in the Iowa plains.

In just under a year, Tom had sharpened his aim until he could clip the tail feathers off a flying sparrow.

He'd actually stood at Niestrom's side during a dozen robberies.

He'd even killed his first man.

That last one still sat in Tom's gut like a bad piece of meat, but it was something he had now which hadn't been there before. It was something that Tom was immensely proud of and it was getting a little easier to digest with each passing day.

Tom wasn't the same person he'd been when he was on that farm. The difference between those two was more than the transition from boy to man. It was more like night and day.

His father had said Tom would go to hell if he followed in Niestrom's footsteps. But what the hell did he know? He was only in a fit of envy, just like everyone else who recognized Thomas Bolander on sight. That's what Niestrom had told him and since he had no reason to doubt his new mentor, Tom took the other man's word as gospel.

They were all just jealous.

Those that weren't jealous were afraid.

The very thought that someone might be afraid of him

made Tom's chest puff out even more. His smile quickly turned into a well-practiced sneer that had been honed to something near perfection. That look was one of the first things Niestrom had taught him. When it was turned toward any of the folks Tom passed on his way out of the hotel, that same sneer caused them to quickly turn away.

"Yeah," Tom thought as he crossed the street. "They damn well better be afraid if they know what's good for 'em."

Tom stepped onto the boardwalk in front of the Yellow Dog and pushed the door open with a strong shove. Once inside, he turned that sneer up to its full power and gazed into the room, waiting for the same fear he'd gotten outside.

Only one person inside the saloon took any notice of Tom's entrance, however, and that man didn't seem the least bit impressed.

"Where the hell have you been?" Niestrom asked in a voice that was slightly tainted by Dave's whiskey.

Trying to salvage some of the pride he'd been building, Tom strutted over to where the gunfighter was standing and took a spot at the bar.

Niestrom's eyes blazed a hole into the side of Tom's skull. The longer he went without hearing from the youth, the more it seemed as if steam was seeping out from between his clenched teeth. "I asked you a question, boy. If you know what's good for you, you'd best answer it."

"I had something to tend to, John. Don't make such a fuss over it."

"You'd best not be talking about that whore you were making eyes at when we first got here."

"And what if I am?" Tom asked with an edge that was just as finely honed as his sneer.

Niestrom let out the breath he'd been holding, stepped up so that he was nose-to-nose with Tom and replied, "Don't try none of your shit with me, kid. In case you forgot, I'm the one that wiped the snot from yer nose and taught you how to stand up for yerself. And if you don't watch your step around me, I can show you how to fall."

All of the confidence that had been keeping Tom's back straight as a board drained out of him right along with most of the color in his face. The young man swallowed hard and fought to direct some of his anger into his bearing. But the only thing that showed in his eyes was fear. Rather than try to hide it, he simply turned his head and nodded.

Niestrom let out a labored groan as well before reaching out to tussle the younger man's hair. "Was she worth it?"

Still feeling the sting of getting scolded, Tom faced the bar and shrugged.

"I asked you a question," Niestrom said in a way that mocked the gruffness of the first time he'd uttered that same thing.

Finally, Tom's anger started to wane and he did his best to hide that fact. But he knew that wouldn't fool Niestrom, so he nodded earnestly and said, "Hell yeah it was worth it."

"Good. In fact, I'm glad you got that out of your system early because we've got a long night ahead of us."

His interest peaked, Tom looked over to Niestrom and asked, "Really? What's going on?"

"The name of the game is poker. But that's not half as good as the name of one of the men we're playing against."

EIGHT

Usually, nothing could ever live up to a fond memory.

After finishing off the last piece of peach pie which had been set aside for him by Sandra, Clint realized that that idea couldn't be more wrong. The sweet aftertaste still hung on his lips like the memory of a kiss and his mouth was still warm from the perfect, flaky crust.

"So how was it?" Sandra asked on her way back through the room after cleaning up a dirty table.

Clint started to say something, but stopped short when he spotted one last bit of pie left on his plate. It was hardly big enough to fill his fork, but he stopped everything just the same and dug into it as though it was a meal in itself. When he tried to talk again, all that came out was a series of muffled syllables.

"I'll take that to mean you liked it," Sandra said. "I told you the cook was a helluva lot better than the last one."

After washing down the absolute last of the pie with a final sip of coffee, Clint dabbed his mouth with his napkin and tossed the scrap of material onto the table. "That was the best slice of pie I've had in a long, long time. And I feel like a robber since I didn't pay for it."

Sandra waved off the comment with a free hand.

"Think nothing of it. In case you haven't noticed, I've been on my feet since before you came in here and nearly every moment since then. Sitting with you was better than lying down next to most other men."

Suddenly, Sandra seemed to be a little embarrassed by what she'd just said. The flush in her cheeks passed quickly, though, and was followed by an endearing smile. "Well . . . let's just say I appreciated the sweet thought."

"If you thought that was sweet, then just wait to see what I can arrange for an encore."

"If I didn't know any better, I'd say you were after more than just a free dessert, Clint."

"You do know better . . . and you're absolutely right. When can you get out of here?"

The reluctant look on Sandra's face came and went in just under three seconds. She tried to keep it up just to seem proper, but she wasn't fooling Clint for a moment.

"Do you know how many men proposition me every day?" she asked.

"For a beautiful woman such as yourself . . . probably quite a few."

After meeting his gaze for a couple seconds to allow her to think, Sandra finally gave in and nodded as her warm smile drifted back into place. "I have to work for another hour or so."

"Then how about you meet me for a drink when you're ready? I'll be at the Yellow Dog for a good part of the night." Clint paused for a moment and added, "In fact, I might even be there for a part of tomorrow morning as well."

That seemed to perk her interest. "Are you playing in the big game Dave's holding at his place tonight?"

Clint's head twitched back a little in surprise. "Yes I am. How did you know about that?"

"A man came in for a quick meal over there," she said while pointing to a small round table in the corner that she'd just finished cleaning. "He seemed awful worked up about something and couldn't wait to impress me with the fact that he'd been invited to a high-stakes game. Come to think of it, he invited me to join him there also."

Clint held up his hands. "Well, if he beat me to the punch, then I should probably step aside."

"Don't you dare. He drops so much money in that place that you'd think he had a hole in his pocket. Dave told me once that he used that one's losses to pay for a new front window." Suddenly, Sandra looked embarrassed and lifted a hand to cover her mouth. "I probably shouldn't have said anything like that, should I?"

Laughing, Clint got up and handed over some money to cover his bill. "If he's as bad as that, it would've probably taken me all of two minutes to figure it out for myself. But thanks for the tip, all the same."

Sandra took the money from him and started to walk toward the kitchen with her hands full of dirty dishes. "I'm looking forward to seeing you, Clint. And good luck with the game."

Clint left the restaurant and stepped out into the fresh air. Although the wintry chill was still present, it didn't have the same bite as it had a month or so ago. All in all, he figured it was a good night for some cards. Especially since it had been a while since he'd sat down to more than a few hands. And there wasn't a better place he could think of in the entire state for a game of poker than the Yellow Dog.

The very prospect made Clint feel like a kid waiting for the sun to come up on Christmas morning.

NINE

Stepping through the front door of the Yellow Dog, Clint had to take a moment to get his bearings. He was sure he'd gone to the right place, but the saloon seemed to have changed dramatically in the short time he'd been gone. Namely, the walls appeared to have been moved in about ten feet or so.

That was mainly due to the fact that just about every square foot of space inside the place was filled with humanity and the air was just as packed with chattering voices and cross-talk. There wasn't a space to be found anywhere near the bar. Dashing back and forth in a frantic pace, Dave couldn't have been happier as he dodged around the two extra helpers he'd called in to help serve the crowd.

Somehow, the barkeep managed to look up at just the right time, spot Clint and start waving his hand as though his fingers had caught on fire. "Mister Adams! Great to see you. Come on over here!"

Letting out a stifled groan, Clint took a step inside the saloon and was immediately set upon by people pushing past him and bumping into him. Only a few of them seemed to have heard what Dave said, but those that did spread the word and soon more than half the eyes in the place were glancing in his direction.

As long as Clint kept moving, he found he could side-step most of the bodies that stumbled across his path. And by the time he'd made it to the bar, he was glad to see that nearly all of those who had been eyeing him had already found something else to gawk at. Thanks to some rather insistent shoving on Dave's part, Clint had a spot where he could place his hands upon the bar.

"What the hell is all of this?" Clint asked as he leaned forward so he didn't have to yell to be heard.

Dave shrugged unconvincingly. "You got me, Mister Adams. These folks just showed up not too long ago. Thursdays are usually busy, but every once in a while they—"

"They what?" Clint interrupted. "They get spiced up by someone advertising a big poker game?"

"I had to put the word out to get players," the barkeep said, looking guilty as sin. "Plus, folks tend to expect a certain show when they come to the Yellow Dog and—"

"Show? So I'm a show now?"

"No, no, of course not, Mister Adams. That was a bad choice of words, but they like to be around for exciting games, at least for the start. Then they always start gambling on their own and everything gets back to normal."

Clint saw that he'd shaken up the bartender a whole lot more than he'd intended, so he let the other man off the hook by patting him on the shoulder and saying, "I just don't think it's a great idea to go around drawing a crowd like this. Especially since I know you'd rather not have any trouble in here."

"Oh, there won't be any trouble. Take a look for yourself."

Sure enough, when Clint took another look, the commotion had died down even more. Although the place was still packed to the rafters, just about everyone inside had

started entertaining themselves and were no longer looking at Clint as though he was the main attraction.

Clint's eyes came to a rest on one of the only places
in the saloon that didn't look as if it had been infested
with life. Sitting in a spot along the back wall, like a
singular oasis of calm, was a round card table with five
seats. Three of those seats were taken already and those
players sat talking amongst themselves. Two were even
playing a game of solitaire just as easy as you please,
conducting themselves as though they were enjoying a
nice day on a friend's front porch.

"That's your table in the back, Mister Adams," Dave
said when he saw where Clint was looking. "I know you
prefer a spot away from the door and along the wall."

If Clint had had to pick the table, out of all the others
in the entire saloon, that would have been the one. He felt
even better about it when he saw that there were no
crowds gathered around the edge of the table like an audience the way that sometimes happened at big games.
Clint wasn't one to be particular about such things, but
he didn't like to start off games like that unless there was
a good reason.

The more he took in the saloon, the more comfortable
Clint became. "The table's fine, Dave. It's just been
awhile since I've played here, that's all."

The barkeep nodded knowingly. "It has, hasn't it? Well,
folks do expect a certain type of company when they
come here and tonight they sure won't be disappointed."

While Dave prattled on about some of his more noto-
rious moments, Clint studied the three people who were
already at his table. One of them looked to be a kid just
shy of his twentieth birthday. There was a rugged, well-
groomed man wearing a jacket cut from the smart blues
of a Federal Officer. And sitting with her back so straight
that it seemed to be nailed to her chair, was a woman
whose face Clint recognized almost immediately.

Normally, Clint had an eye for beautiful women and prided himself on remembering each one of them. And though he certainly remembered this woman, it wasn't because of her beauty. On the contrary, this particular face wouldn't have even looked good on a man, but at least it would have looked more at home there.

A tuft of dark hair hung down from a wide-brimmed hat, framing a severe, rough-looking face. She wore a dark-brown dress buttoned all the way up to her neck, covering up a figure that was probably best left unseen. Clint didn't have to see the petite holster to know that it would be hanging around her waist, just as he knew the dainty revolver it carried.

"Is that Belle Starr?" Clint asked, more as a formality than out of curiosity.

Dave nodded like a proud poppa. "Yessir, it sure is. She came into town on her way back out West. Decided to stop in for a game and paid me a visit. I think it must be fate."

"Yeah, well just make sure someone's watching the horses out front. Is Sam around?"

"Mister Starr's around here somewhere. Can I set you up with a beer before you play? It's on the house."

Clint smirked and said, "With all this business we're bringing in, drinks better be free for the whole table."

"I'll see to it," Dave replied.

After accepting his mug from the barkeep, Clint tipped his hat in gratitude and made his way across the crowded room. Several of the locals offered their greetings and everyone seemed friendly enough. They stepped aside and didn't treat him at all the way he'd expected. In fact, Clint was almost to his table when he realized that most of his first impressions had been completely wrong.

Some of the folks looked as though they knew who he was, but didn't pay him any more mind than that. What little bits and pieces of conversations that he could pick up along the way told Clint that the poker game was very much anticipated, but only as a side note. Mostly, the saloon was filled with other gamblers and card sharps looking to take advantage of the big crowd to do some fleecing of their own.

What had thrown Clint off the most was just how much the Yellow Dog had grown. More than just a place known among a certain group of people, the place had acquired some wider renown of its own. That didn't take away from its charm, however, and when Clint finally claimed a seat at the table against the rear wall, he felt at home once again.

"Who's ready to play some poker?" Clint said by way of introduction.

TEN

At first, Tom didn't notice the new arrival at the table. He was still too starry-eyed from swapping stories with Belle Starr and giving a hard time to Sergeant Allman, who seemed so out of his element that it was almost funny. When the tall, simply dressed man sat down in one of the two remaining chairs, Tom's first impulse was to shoo him away just as he'd had to do when any of the other locals had tried to sit in.

But before he could snarl out the gruff warning, Tom was stopped by the voice of the unattractive woman sitting to his left.

"Hello there, Mister Adams," Belle said while offering her hand like a proper lady rather than the horse thief and cattle rustler she was. "It's good to see you under such . . . friendly circumstances."

Clint settled into the chair and placed his beer on the table in front of him. "How do you do, Belle?" he replied, taking her hand and shaking it cordially. "I was surprised to see you here. Especially after what happened in . . . Oklahoma, wasn't it?"

Belle smiled in a way that still somehow completely failed to soften her features. Instead, she simply looked like a rugged cowhand trying to look attractive in a hat and petticoat. "If you're referring to my time in jail, I served that and was released."

"Actually, I was talking about your appearance before Judge Isaac Parker." Snapping his fingers, Clint winced and said, "Wait a minute, he's in Fort Smith isn't he?"

Nodding while fixing her eyes upon Clint in much the same way she might if she was staring at him over the barrel of her gun, she said, "Yes, he is. And that case was dismissed."

Clint was actually starting to have some fun here. "Dismissed? 'Hanging Judge' Parker dismissed your case?"

"Lack of evidence," Belle snorted.

"I see. Well, that was a lucky break for you. And so you decided to celebrate by playing a few games of cards with some old friends."

"I'll settle for whoever wants to join me. I'm not much of a gambler, but I do enjoy the occasional hand or two."

"Pick up some extra money after getting chased out of one state from another?"

Belle's hand drifted toward her holster and her eyes looked as though they'd been covered over with a layer of ice. "Did I wrong you sometime, Mister Adams? Or are you like this with all the ladies you meet in places like this?"

It wasn't easy, but Clint was able to keep from questioning where Belle fit on the "lady" scale. Instead, he shrugged and raised his hands in surrender. "You've got me there, Belle. I apologize."

Clint picked out one face from the crowd which had been taking an intense interest in what was going on at the table. He was a rough-looking man with dark-red skin and the scowl of someone just looking for an excuse to start breaking something apart. Clint hadn't met him personally, but his best guess was that the man was Belle's husband, Sam Starr.

Sam, a Cherokee Indian, had married Belle and had been with her ever since on several strings of robberies spanning just as many states. The big Indian was just starting to make his way toward the back of the room when he locked eyes with Clint.

Glancing over her shoulder, Belle spotted the Cherokee and said, "It's all right, Sam. Mister Adams is just having some fun with me. Cole always said he was a pleasant sort."

Clint had crossed paths with Cole Younger once or twice in the past, but the experiences weren't exactly what he might have called pleasant. Despite that fact, the Cherokee didn't know that and appeared to be satisfied with the explanation. He shot Clint one more warning look and turned to go back to the bar.

Even though Clint preferred to stay on the right side of the law, he was able to get along with those who strayed from that path so long as they treated him with respect. He'd met up with just as many unsavory types that had turned out all right as he had with lawmen who'd turned out to be snakes with badges. With that in mind, he decided to let up on Belle Starr for the time being. He'd tested her enough to get a feel for her personality and it was time to move on to the rest of the players.

"So Cole said I was a pleasant sort, huh?" Clint asked once Sam was well out of earshot.

Belle grinned unattractively and replied, "Not at all. Sam just gets a bit overprotective."

Deciding to let that sit where it had landed, Clint turned toward the man on his right. "And what brings you here this fine evening?"

The man sitting there wore his dark-blond hair long for a soldier, which Clint figured either meant he was retired or serving somewhere out of his superiors' reach. "I won't lie to you, sir. I've known Dave for some time and he owes me a fair amount of favors. When I heard about this game, I cashed some in and got myself a seat. Hope you don't mind."

"The only way I would mind is if you couldn't pay up when you lose," Clint said with a lighthearted smile.

The soldier took the comment exactly as it was intended and started laughing heartily. "Sergeant Allman," he said while extending his hand.

Clint accepted the greeting and introduced himself as well. "Nice to meet you."

Tom watched all of these exchanges and formed his own opinion about the new arrival. The first thing he concluded was that this couldn't possibly be the Clint Adams he'd heard so much about.

And almost as if he could sense the thoughts running through the kid's head, Clint turned toward Tom and gave an offhanded wave. "And what about you?" he asked. "Are you a friend of Dave's as well?"

Before Tom could answer, he felt a hand slap him on the back of his shoulder.

"No," said John Niestrom as he walked around and took the chair between Belle and Allman. "He's a friend of mine."

ELEVEN

Niestrom took his seat and nodded his greetings to the rest of the players. He nodded to all of them except for Tom, that is. To the kid, he gave a sly grin and folded his hands in front of him on the table. "I was surprised you'd show up, Adams."

Clint could tell what kind of a man this was the instant he'd first exchanged words with him. But just to give him his moment in the sun, he decided to provide the opening Niestrom had been waiting for and asked, "Why's that?"

"Seeing as how quickly you skinned out of here a while ago, it looked to me like you might not be coming back."

Even though Clint had been trading barbed comments with Belle Starr and hassling the kid every now and then, everything he'd said had been taken in stride. Belle didn't look any more offended as she had when Clint had arrived and even she seemed taken aback by Niestrom's sudden attitude.

Clint hadn't expected any less from the gunfighter and didn't give Niestrom the satisfaction of seeing him react to his words. Instead, Clint let the insult hang in the air for a couple of moments before leaning forward slightly in his chair.

44

"All I'm here for is a game of poker," Clint said. "If you want to start something, do it right now so I can put you down and then get on with the game."

"Oh, you want to try me, is that it Adams?"

"Not really. But that's up to you. So either start what you want to start or shut your hole so we can get on with this."

Tom glanced nervously between Clint and Niestrom, half expecting either man to draw his gun. After a couple of seconds, it became obvious that neither one of them was about to shoot the other, which caused the hairs on the back of Tom's neck to lie back down against his skin.

"Fine," Niestrom said calmly. "Just thought I'd clear the air between us to make sure we could have a nice civil game."

"That's the least of your worries," Clint said. "If I were you, I'd be more concerned about losing the shirt off my back before this night is through."

Once again, the tension seemed to crackle in the air. Sergeant Allman wore the stern face of a born disciplinarian, and Belle looked as though she were watching a stage show. Tom was starting to get fidgety again and his hand drifted down toward the gun at his side.

Suddenly, Niestrom broke into a hoarse kind of laughter, slapping the table in front of him with the palm of his hand. "We'll see about that, Adams. We will definitely see about that."

And then everyone else at the table was fairly sure they weren't about to be in the middle of crossfire. The mood around the five players shifted to match the jovial mood filling the rest of the saloon. Sergeant Allman seemed more relieved than any of them for the change.

"Now that we're all here," the officer stated. "Let's get down to business."

After sweeping in the cards he'd been using to play solitaire, the Army man stacked them together and started shuffling. He was halfway through the second shuffle when Niestrom reached out with his left hand and stopped the cards dead.

"Get a new deck," the gunfighter said.

Clearly offended by the insinuation, Allman replied, "I beg your pardon?"

"You heard me, General. I don't know where the hell them cards have been so you can get some new ones."

Tom knew only too well that Niestrom wasn't joking. Rather than have another exchange of threats, he got up and grabbed his empty mug. "I'll get some from Dave. I have to get some more beer anyway."

More than happy to excuse himself for a moment, Tom pushed away from the table and started wading through the crowd on his way to the bar. He made it about halfway before he spotted another familiar face among all the gamblers and drunks.

Abby's smile shone through the entire saloon like a ray of sunshine. It wasn't so much that he felt strongly for her, but Tom was just plain relieved to get his mind on something as pleasant as the last time he'd spent with Abby.

"Looking for these?" Abby asked while holding out a fresh deck of cards.

The look of surprise on Tom's face must have been pretty good because it certainly brought a decent laugh from Abby.

"How'd you know I was coming for those?" he asked.

Abby stepped forward and tossed the cards into Tom's hands. "I didn't. Dave sent me over to deliver them to you. He said something about some half-brained Army man messing with the pack he'd left there before. You gamblers are so superstitious."

"Superstition's got nothing to do with it," Tom replied. "John just don't like cheaters."

"Not unless he's the one marking the deck, right?"

"I don't know you well enough to have you talk about John like that. He's taught me a lot."

Sidling up a little closer, Abby reached down and brushed her hands between his legs. "If he taught you everything you know, then maybe I shared my bed with the wrong man."

Even though they were too close together for anyone else to see where Abby's hands were, Tom looked around as if one of the nearby gamblers actually cared about what he was doing. "You want to watch me play?" he asked, regaining the boastful tone in his voice.

"Maybe."

Tom took that as a definite "yes" and winked at the brunette. With that, he turned sharply on his heels and headed back toward the table.

Watching him leave, Abby couldn't help but be amused by the kid's arrogance. She waited for him to look back at her over his shoulder. When the glance finally came, she smiled convincingly, blew him a kiss and waved.

"Stupid boy," Abby whispered once Tom found his seat. "Stupid, stupid boy."

TWELVE

Belle might not have been much of a gambler, but she knew her way around a game of poker well enough to rake in the first couple of pots. Since he usually took it easy the first couple of hands anyway, Clint didn't mind seeing her claim the first couple of victories.

For Clint, the first hour or so of a long poker game was like the initial rounds of a boxing match. The fighters circled each other for a bit, took a couple jabs when the time was right, but didn't bother wasting any haymakers. It was more important to size up the opposition and try to figure out their style rather than charge blindly into what might very well be the first and only mistake of the game.

Some people didn't care too much for such tactics when they bellied up to a card table. Clint knew that those kind of people would never be gamblers. The only thing they were good for was lining a real player's pockets.

What most normal folks might consider work, Clint thought of as downright relaxing. It soothed his brain to sit back and figure out cold odds and try to work up what he thought the other players were holding. After all, unlike most of life's true challenges, a man could take his time in a poker game and do things right.

Clint knew only too well that he wouldn't get a chance like this too often and when he did, he figured on taking full advantage of it. As far as he could tell, Sergeant Allman was the easiest of the players to figure out. Being a military man, he wasn't all that good at bluffing and tended to make bold plays when he had the firepower to back them up.

The kid was next on Clint's list. Tom might have had some good moves, but he didn't have the experience to know exactly when to make them. And he was still a bit timid when push came to shove, a problem that would be solved with age. Clint decided to keep an eye on him all the same, since the kid would probably come up with a trick or two before the night was out.

Then there was Belle. So far, she seemed to have been telling the truth when she said she wasn't much of a gambler. She'd pulled off a few hands, but that could have been just as much luck as anything resembling skill. Although she seemed overly happy when she did win, she was hanging on a bit too well to be a beginner. The main thing putting Clint's mind at ease was the fact that she was a known woman. If she was any kind of threat at a poker game, Clint would have heard about it. Lord knows he heard plenty of other things about her.

It was Clint's turn to deal. "Five Card Stud," he announced. As he flipped the cards to each player, his mind centered on the man sitting more or less directly in front of him. So far, Clint could count on one hand the number of times that Niestrom had taken his eyes off of him. Not that the gunfighter was disturbing him. On the contrary, Clint was so used to getting those looks from men like Niestrom that he only got uncomfortable when they didn't come.

But that's not to say that Clint enjoyed being the center

of Niestrom's attention. He may not have been a mind reader, but Clint had a pretty good idea of what was traveling through that one's skull. And at least part of what was occupying Niestrom's brain had something to do with the kid named Tom.

From time to time, those two exchanged looks that were ripe with meaning, and none of it seemed all that good. As for Niestrom's poker playing abilities, he had a fair amount of skill and knew well enough not to display too much of it right away. So rather than bother himself too much with trying to figure Niestrom out, Clint decided to sit back and just play the game.

It wouldn't be long before a man like Niestrom got impatient and tipped his hand.

Looking to the man on his left, Clint asked, "What'll it be, Tom?"

The kid peeked at his down card and scowled for a few moments. "Check."

Clint hadn't expected anything less, since Tom hadn't placed the first bet of any hand since the game had started.

Next in line was Belle. Just for fun, Clint tried to predict what she might do. He decided that since she'd been starting to play things a little closer to the vest now that she'd built up some stacks in front of her, Belle might start trying to draw more bets in rather than shoot for the big win right away.

"Count me in for twenty dollars," Belle announced with an ugly smirk. She wasn't exactly trying to look menacing, but that was the only kind of smirk her face was capable of.

Clint shook his head almost imperceptibly. Either Belle was bluffing as she thought she had one hell of a hand. Either way, she'd probably just scared away the Sergeant and he was the man with the most cash to burn.

Locking eyes with Clint, Niestrom didn't even glance

toward his cards before tossing in the right amount of chips. "I'm in for that and five more."

Clint truly loved playing cards with men who had something to prove. They were the easiest ones to read as far as the game went, but the tricky part was always in what it was they were truly trying to accomplish. For now, he just waited patiently.

The Sergeant looked at his cards and then up to Belle. Back at his cards, then to Niestrom. After one more glance at his cards and a sweeping stare that covered both Clint and Tom, he said, "Fold."

If Clint was in this for the money, he would've been plenty mad at Belle right then. But he was sitting here for fun and Niestrom alone was proving to be an amusing distraction.

"I'm in," Clint said while tossing in twenty-five dollars in chips.

Both Tom and Belle accepted the raise and Clint dealt another card up to each of the remaining players. This time, Tom threw in for a couple dollars, only to be immediately raised by Belle. The fleeting, anguished look on Tom's face was all Clint needed to see to know that the kid wasn't holding much of anything. To Tom's credit, though, his face turned stony enough after that first slip. He'd probably make a fairly good card player . . . in about five or six years.

Once again, Niestrom stayed true to form. "Raise another ten," he said in a cocky tone while fixing Clint with a challenging stare.

The only one who seemed impressed with the gunfighter was Sergeant Allman. His bushy eyebrows twitched slightly and he grunted under his breath while turning to look for Clint's reaction.

Everyone called and Clint dealt out the fifth card. The game moved along as it had before, the kid betting a small amount, Belle, raising, and then Neistrom raising again, this time twenty.

Clint already knew exactly what he wanted to do. But rather than move right ahead, he decided to play the moment out for a bit longer just to see how Niestrom would react.

First, he leaned back in his chair and pretended to study his hold card intently. Lying in front of him was the nine and ten of diamonds, the ten of hearts and the eight of spades. Niestrom was showing a pair of queens, the seven of hearts and the ace of clubs. Clint made a move for his chips, pulled back, reached out again, and retracted his hand after a moment or two of thought.

Tom was getting impatient with every second that passed. And even though Clint hadn't been paying the kid much mind, that fact was clear enough to sense without him even looking in the young man's direction. Throughout Clint's entire display, Niestrom didn't move a muscle. In fact, he became more still every time Clint seemed to be changing his mind until the gunfighter resembled a statue that had been built for the sole purpose of filling a seat.

Finally, just to clear the table of Tom and possibly Belle, Clint let his indecisive charade drop away to leave his face cold as the steel of his modified Colt. "Raise a hundred," he said while pushing in most of his chips.

THIRTEEN

As predicted, Tom dropped faster than an anvil off a cliff with Belle not too far behind. Niestrom looked as though he was about to charge over the table and wrap his hands around Clint's neck.

"You trying to show me up, Adams?" Niestrom asked.

Clint sat back, but didn't let the edge in his eyes dull in the slightest. "I've heard of you, Niestrom. They call you Third Eye, don't they?"

Unable to hold back the surge of pride that flooded through him at that moment, Niestrom replied, "Yeah. Anyone I don't take to gets a third eye for their troubles. Right here," he added while tapping the center of his forehead with his index finger.

"Maybe you should stay out of poker games, Third Eye. A temper like that doesn't float too well in a friendly game of cards."

"Is that a fact?"

Clint could sense the other man was quickly approaching his limit. And though it would have been just as easy to back off and let Niestrom cool down, he reminded himself that he was at this table for a good time. Appeasing someone like Niestrom just didn't fit too well in that respect.

"If you're trying to prove something," Clint said in a steady voice. "Then go ahead and prove it. You can start by proving whether or not you're a smart gambler by making up your mind about what to do with the bet that's on the table. In or out, Third Eye. Let's have it."

For the first time that Clint had noticed since the game began, Niestrom looked away rather than keep eye contact with him. It was only for a split second, but Niestrom's eyes darted down to his cards and then flicked right back up to fix upon Clint. From there, he glanced over to Tom.

Following the gunfighter's lead, Clint looked over to the kid as well and found Tom to be anxiously awaiting the outcome of this bet. More than that, he seemed to be hanging on the edge of his chair.

It took another long second for him to make up his mind, but Niestrom walked down the exact path that Clint had predicted. "Call," he said while shoving all but his smallest stack onto the middle of the table. "You're bluffing, Adams. I can see the pile of shit building up behind your eyes."

"Really?" Clint said while tossing the nine of clubs next to its companion and the pair of tens. "Must be the glare."

For a moment, time itself seemed to grind to a halt. Clint kept still since his right hand was already within drawing distance of his Colt. Tom looked almost as stunned as the sergeant and Belle clapped her hands upon the table and held them there.

Niestrom's only movement was a tic in his left eye. The overconfident smirk still hung on his face like a smudge left from a grease fire, and the tip of his tongue flicked out to wet the edge of his bottom lip. When his hand started to slowly creep off the table, everyone there tensed in anticipation. Belle, especially, seemed ready for

a violent move since that was much more in her line of
business than the finer aspects of poker.

But Niestrom stopped his hand right before it dropped
out of sight. From there, he tossed down his hold card
while his lips parted to bare his teeth. The third queen
landed in front of the jagged line of his four other cards
and was announced by a collective gasp from the other
three observers.

"Choke on her, Adams," Niestrom sneered. "And then
shove all three of 'em up yer ass."

Clint looked at all the cards on the table, nodded, and
held his hands up to the pot as if to offer it safe passage.
"You got me," he said calmly. "And might I congratulate
you on being such a gracious winner."

Niestrom either chose to ignore the sarcasm in Clint's
voice or didn't even catch it to begin with. Either way,
he was too busy making a show of collecting his winnings
and playing it up to the rest of the people at the table. He
even waved once toward the bar, even though nobody else
seemed to be paying him much attention.

"Drinks are on me," Niestrom said, without noticing
that Clint had already signalled the barkeep.

Less than a second or two after that announcement,
Abby walked up to the table with a tray full of full beer
glasses. She set them down in front of each player and
relieved them of their empties. "Compliments of Mister
Adams," she said sweetly and then turned to head back
toward the bar.

Belle and Sergeant Allman lifted their drinks and sa-
luted Clint happily. With the tension lifted, they started
talking about the game as well as that last hand with the
man who'd lost the pot while completely ignoring the
winner.

Even though he was currently sitting behind the largest
stack of chips at the table, Niestrom quickly realized that
he'd been bumped out of the spotlight just as quickly as

he'd stepped into it. "I need a word with you, Tom," he said while getting up and stalking toward the door.

If anyone noticed the absence of the pair, neither of the three who stayed behind felt compelled to break the flow of their banter to mention it.

FOURTEEN

Most of the games that were taking place near the main table had stopped so the others could get a look at what happened during that last hand. Those who were still watching when Niestrom got up to leave nodded in approval at the gunfighter's victory. Some of them even offered up a word or two of congratulations.

But Niestrom wasn't having any of it. Despite the fact that he'd won the hand, he still felt a sting beneath his skin and the twitching in his eye had yet to let up.

Even Dave had something to say when Niestrom passed the bar, but his words were lost amid the incessant rushing going through the other man's ears. Niestrom got to the front door, pulled it open hard enough for the handle to put a dent in the wall and stormed outside.

Tom stepped outside a few seconds behind him. The moment he got into the open air, the younger man let out a deep breath followed by a victorious holler.

"What're you so fucking happy about?" Niestrom asked. He was standing on the edge of the boardwalk, gazing out into the inky night with his hands folded tightly across his chest.

Tom looked a little confused by the question. Then

57

again, he'd gotten used to the gunfighter reacting in odd ways. This time, however, he wasn't at all surprised at the tantrum. "You won, John. And that was a hell of a lot of money!"

"So? Who gives a damn about the money? The money wasn't the point of what happened in there. Or are you just too stupid to realize that?"

"I ain't stupid," Tom said, his face and tone reflecting a newfound seriousness.

"Well you could'a fooled me the way you were carrying on just now. You'd better hope that nobody else saw you actin' like some goddamn schoolboy who won a round of mumblety-peg." Whipping around to face the younger man, Niestrom pounded across the loosely fitted wooden slats until he was close enough to butt heads with Tom. "Haven't you listened to a damn word I've been telling you all this time?"

"Yeah, John. I've been—"

"Then how come you haven't been taking advantage of this opportunity I've given you? How come you've been watching me more than you've been watching who you should be?"

Tom thought for a second. "You mean Belle Starr?"

Niestrom's hand lashed out so quickly that Tom didn't think to flinch before he felt the impact of it smacking against the side of his head. The kid's hat toppled off and before it landed on the ground, the .44 was in his fist and jabbing into Niestrom's gut.

The older gunfighter stared into Tom's eyes and nodded approvingly. "Good," he said without seeming too concerned about the pistol barrel stuck beneath his ribs. "Now you're finally starting to get on the ball."

Tom's thumb was still poised on the .44's hammer and aching to snap it back into firing position. What he did instead was pull the gun away and drop it into his holster. "Don't treat me like that," he warned. Stooping to retrieve his hat, he raised himself back up and glared at Niestrom in a way that would have made many men think twice about saying another word.

Niestrom, however, simply smiled a little wider. "*That's* what I like about you, kid. I was starting to forget why I took you under my wing." Acting as though nothing at all had gone wrong, Niestrom reached out and draped his arm over Tom's shoulder. "We're not here to play cards. This here is a lesson you've got to learn or else you ain't ever going to be known for anything outside of this town.

"I had to smack some sense into that head of yours because you were talking crazy. Belle Starr is just a horse thief who got lucky a few times. She ain't even a very good horse thief because she keeps landing in jail."

"She's killed men," Tom said in his defense. "I hear she's even good with that iron she carries. And she's known."

"Sure she's known. She's known for being uglier than the horses she's so fond of stealing. Hell, the men she killed probably couldn't stand to look in her eyes for very long and that's how she got the drop on them. The one you'd best be watching is Adams."

By the look on Tom's face, one might have thought that Niestrom had suggested walking up to the devil himself and throwing down. "You think I'm ready to take on Clint Adams?"

"It don't matter what I think. What matters is that you make yerself seen and heard when you're around someone like that. If you want to be a bad man, you've got to make a name for yourself. A name is what folks remember. And a man gets a name by butting heads with them that're higher up on the totem pole."

Tom took a deep breath, held it and then let it out. "I don't know about that, John."

"You don't know?" Niestrom asked in a voice dripping

with poison. "Then hang up yer gun right now and start buying up some land. Maybe you can start a nice farm like yer poppa and you can spend the rest of your days shoveling pig shit for a living. Does that sound good to you?"

His chin lowered, Tom shook his head.

"Do you trust what I have to say?" Niestrom asked.

Still looking down, Tom nodded.

After a moment's hesitation, Niestrom said, "I wouldn't steer you wrong, kid. If you want to start building a life for yourself, you can make a big step right here, right now. And if you're not willing to go up against the likes of Clint Adams, then you don't belong in this game at all."

Steeling himself, Tom rested his hand upon the handle of his gun and put on the grim mask he'd practiced for so long. "You're right."

"Of course I am. Now when we go back in there, I want you to make up your mind. Either walk away . . . or throw in your ante. There ain't no other choices."

In his mind, Tom had already made his decision. "I still got an ace in the hole to play and it might be just the type of ace that can get me a decent shot at that Gunsmith."

Niestrom was intrigued. "Is that so?"

"Yeah. Adams is supposed to be a ladies' man isn't he?"

FIFTEEN

"Well, well, well. If it isn't Clint Adams himself."

When it became clear that Tom and Niestrom weren't about to come right back from their little walk, Clint had decided to get up and stretch his own legs. According to the clock on the wall above the bar, it had been two and a half hours since he'd first sat down. To him, it hardly felt like twenty minutes.

Standing at the end of the bar, Clint had been just about ready to ask for a refill of his beer when he heard those words come at him from behind. The speaker's voice was soft, feminine and vaguely familiar. He turned around to get a look and was instantly glad that he did.

"How you doing, Abby?" Clint asked when he saw the shapely brunette step up to him. "For a moment I thought you were about to ignore me for the rest of the night since you didn't seem to notice me the first time you walked by."

"It's not easy ignoring a fine man like you," she said with a sexy grin. "If I wasn't at work, I'd have been all over you and you might have missed out on your game."

Clint laughed once beneath his breath. "That might not

61

have been a bad thing. I would at least have some more money in my pocket."

Wincing dramatically, Abby said, "I saw what happened on that last hand. Folks'll be talking about that for a while."

"And when they stop, I'm sure Dave will remind them until the amount I lost mysteriously goes up by a thousand dollars or so."

Abby tried to cover the way she was giggling since Dave was actually not too far away. She covered her mouth with her hand until she saw that Dave was no longer looking in her direction. "He does like a good story."

"Speaking of good stories, the last time I was in town, you told me that you were all set to go out to California. In fact, didn't I use your nest egg in a poker game back then to get you enough money for the trip?"

"You sure did," Abby replied happily. "Tripled my life savings." Stepping up until she was close enough for her body to brush up against Clint's, she asked, "Did I ever tell you how much I appreciated what you did for me?"

With the brunette so close, Clint could smell the faint sweetness of her hair and could feel the warmth pouring from her skin. Abby was wearing a form-fitting black dress that buttoned straight down the center. She'd stopped buttoning at a point just above her knees, however, which allowed him to see a peek of smooth skin over the tops of her black leather boots.

"As I recall," he said, "you thanked me several times that night. As well as a time or two the next morning."

The color on Abby's cheeks was more of an excited flush rather than any kind of embarrassed reaction. "I'm free tonight if you think I still owe you some thanks."

"Believe me, I'm tempted. But I may be busy tonight," Clint said while nodding toward the table where Sergeant Allman sat alone playing solitaire.

"You're still in the game?"

"I lost that hand, but I'm far from done."

Abby's face showed more than a little concern when she looked over there. By the time she looked back at Clint, she seemed downright worried. "Maybe you should be done with that game."

Holding his hands out to indicate the rest of the saloon around him, Clint said, "And disappoint all my fans after Dave took all that trouble to bring them here? Not on your life."

What made that seem even funnier was the fact that nobody else in the place seemed to even remember that Clint was there anymore. They all went about their games without a care in the world, which was just fine by Clint.

Abby looked around the saloon a couple of times, noticed the apathy of the gamblers, and started to laugh. Just like she did when she was talking about Dave, she tried to cover up her mouth with her hand. Once she'd gotten herself under control, she said, "I think your fans have already gone on to bigger and better things."

"Oh well. I didn't do too well on center stage anyway."

The humor lingered on Abby's face for another moment or two before fading out like light from a candle that had been snuffed.

"What's the matter?" Clint asked. "You seem like something's troubling you."

"I wasn't kidding about that game, Clint. You should get out before you lose more than your money."

"Do you mean Niestrom? There's men like him at every table. If he gets out of line, I can handle him."

"It's not him." Abby paused and glanced over toward the front door. She studied that part of the saloon as well as the faces of the men lingering around that area. "It's Tom you should be worried about," she said in a hushed tone.

SIXTEEN

That one genuinely surprised Clint. "The kid?"

"Yes, the kid. He's not trying to be some kind of gambler and he surely doesn't travel with a man like Niestrom for the company."

"How well do you know that kid?"

"Well enough to know what I'm talking about."

Clint fixed her with a steady gaze that seemed to bore all the way through and out the back of her skull. There was no anger or coldness in his eyes, but he was able to make Abby start squirming a bit and shift on her feet.

Once his eyes became too uncomfortable on her, she stomped one foot and said, "All right, all right. I spent some time with him. And before you ask, yes it was *that kind* of time." She looked into his eyes again to find that they were much warmer now that she'd started opening up to him a little more. "I thought he was . . . interesting."

Clint laughed subtly. "I remember that what you find interesting usually involves carrying a gun and knowing how to use it."

"He was interesting," she said in a way that both ignored and affirmed what Clint had said. "He talked to me about all the . . . jobs he'd done and all the places he'd been. He seemed like a wild boy and so I showed him a couple things."

"*You* showed *him*?"

"Well, he didn't seem knowledgeable about everything, but he was easy enough to teach. Anyway . . . afterward, we were talking and he sounded like he was a little wilder than I thought."

"How so?"

Abby went over the time she'd spent with Tom again in her mind. The longer she thought about some parts of it, the more uncomfortable she started to feel. "I've been with plenty of gunmen before, Clint. After awhile, a girl can start to tell things about a man like that. Things that she may not like to see or even know, but she can't help seeing either way."

"Try to be a little more specific, Abby," Clint said as he glanced about the room. His eyes moved toward the front door as well and he calmly looked away. "We don't have much time. That wild boy of yours just walked back inside."

"Niestrom is teaching him," she said quickly. "I think he's killed a man or two . . . maybe he just got close . . . but it's never been on purpose. The way he talks about it . . . I just can tell he hasn't killed a man in a straight fight."

Oddly enough, Clint knew exactly what Abby was talking about. He'd heard that same tone of voice from countless blowhards bragging to anyone who would listen at their local saloon. They talked and talked and kept right on talking about how bad they were, while anyone who knew what it was to live by the gun knew such men were full of shit.

"I listened to him for a while," she continued. "But I didn't really believe him. I thought that someday he might amount to something and make a name for himself, but he has a ways to go yet. What bothered me was that I could tell he was ready to take that next step and start killing." Abby's eyes looked genuinely troubled when she specified, "*Real* killing."

"Dead is dead," Clint replied. "You're talking about murder instead of getting in a lucky shot during some holdup."

She nodded. "He's ready to kill a man for no better reason than to prove that he can. Don't ask me how I know, Clint, because I just do. And when I saw him here I could tell he might be thinking of a way out of it, but now that Niestrom took him aside, I can only imagine what he's telling him."

Clint could feel the desperation seeping into Abby's voice. The more she tried to say, the quicker she tried to say it. Her frantic pace only quickened when she looked around and spotted Tom and Niestrom making their way back to the card table.

"Be careful of him, Clint. Please."

"You're not the only one who's ever had to deal with these types before, you know. I've actually run across men like Niestrom and Tom myself."

The only response Abby gave to that was a smack of her hand on Clint's shoulder. "All I'm trying to do is warn you and I get nothing but back-talk for my troubles."

"Actually, I was getting a pretty good idea about what was going on with those two. Niestrom might be an all right poker player, but the kid has a lot to learn. What you just said put everything straight."

Hearing that she was actually of some help to him brightened Abby's mood considerably. That brightness faded almost instantly when she noticed that both Niestrom and Tom were taking turns scouting the room for them. Both of the men spotted her and Clint at roughly the same time, but they didn't approach.

"You just remember what I told you," she said while jabbing her finger against Clint's chest. "Plenty of those third eyes that Niestrom is so famous for wound up in the back of men's heads."

Clint nodded. "That's good to know." Pulling Abby a little closer, he leaned down and kissed her gently on the cheek. "Thanks again for all your help."

She started to back away, but decided against it before she'd taken her second step. Abby took hold of Clint's face and pressed her soft, full lips against his, kissing him passionately and allowing the tip of her tongue to flick against his.

Without another word, she turned on the balls of her feet and walked lightly away. Clint was left with a spinning feeling in his stomach which he remembered distinctly from the last time he and Abby had spent time together. When he thought about those steamy nights, he had to force himself to get his mind back on the present situation or he would have been tempted to ditch the poker game altogether.

Glancing over to the table, Clint saw that everyone else was gathered there and ready to go. For the most part, they seemed to be talking quietly amongst themselves. Even Niestrom was chatting sociably with Belle Starr. Tom, however, was everything but calm.

He was turned in his seat and glaring at Clint with a look that burned across the room to focus into two points of heat that bore straight through Clint's eyes. In return, Clint waved casually and started walking through the crowd.

"Oh yeah," he said to himself. "This game should be very interesting indeed."

SEVENTEEN

"I raise another five."

This had been the third raise Tom made in as many rounds of betting. After his private discussion with Niestrom, he seemed to be fired up about something. No matter how much he won or lost, his face never broke from the stern mask that held his features in its stony grip. And whenever possible, he stared at Clint as though he was about to try and kill him at any second.

Surprisingly enough, this intensity had translated into a fairly good run of wins for the kid. Belle and Sergeant Allman were scared off easily enough when he would raise one time after another and Niestrom didn't seem anxious to outplay his pupil.

In fact, Niestrom beamed proudly whenever Tom raked in a pot. He beamed even brighter when Tom managed to win after whittling the players down to just himself and Clint.

Clint watched all of this with a passive, slightly apathetic expression. When he lost, he made only slightly less fuss than when he won. All the while, he kept up the conversation between himself and the other players, not including Tom because the kid simply didn't talk whenever anyone but Niestrom asked him a question.

Despite whatever preconceptions he might have had, Clint actually grew to like talking to Belle. She might not have been too pleasant to look at, but she had plenty of interesting tales to tell and was truly at the table to enjoy playing. That was always a refreshing change when compared to the dry tenseness which filled the air between professional gamblers who took every card as though their life depended on it.

The hours passed like this until the crowd at the Yellow Dog started to thin out a bit. Once that happened, Clint knew it must be getting close to dawn.

"What time is it?" he asked while leaning back in his chair and stretching his legs.

Sergeant Allman plucked a dented brass watch from the pocket of his jacket and flipped open the cover. "Good lord," he said as his eyebrows raised high on his forehead. "It's half past five."

Allman seemed to be the only one affected by this news in the slightest.

Clint looked around and saw that only about half of the tables were filled and there were more spaces at the bar than he'd ever seen. The smell of frying eggs drifted through the room, but it was far from appetizing. The Yellow Dog might have been known for many things, but its cook was not one of them.

Tom smacked his hand down impatiently on the top of the table. "I made a raise, goddammit! That don't mean it's time for you all to start checking your watches."

At the beginning of the game, the rest of the players might have been surprised with such an outburst coming from the kid. But after seeing Tom in action over the last several hours, not a one of them raised more than an eyebrow.

"Fine, I'll see your five," Belle said, looking at the kid

over a possible straight. "And I'll bump it another five just to keep things interesting."

Niestrom scratched his chin and glanced down at the pair of threes showing. All that was left of the game was this round of bets since all cards had been dealt. "Ten to me?" After another second of consideration, he said, "Not worth it," and chucked his card onto the table.

Sergeant Allman was sitting proudly with a row of four clubs spread out in front of him. Playing up the value of his hand with a cocky smile, the military man tossed in some chips. "I'm in."

Clint wasn't too worried about Allman, especially since the Sergeant always smiled that way whenever he was trying to bluff. Turning to look at the other side of the table, he studied the two remaining players.

Belle was a hard one to read. But she normally didn't push things higher than another buck or two unless she really had something to back it up. The kid, on the other hand, might be trying to pull just about anything.

Deciding that the best way to see what Tom was trying this time would be the direct approach, Clint placed his hold card facedown beneath his hand and fixed the kid with a hard stare. For a second, Tom kept the fire in his eyes burning brightly. But it didn't hold up much longer than that before he blinked and looked away.

"So what the hell are you about to do, Adams?" Tom asked once he lifted his eyes back into position. "Put up or shut up."

Clint's cards were set up in a neat row. Two fives and another pair of eights. He was through looking at his own hand, however, and acted as though it no longer even existed. Without letting his eyes drift from Tom's, he reached down and grabbed a stack of chips. "Raise twenty-five."

Tom counted out the right amount of chips from his messy pile and shoved them forward. "And another five."

Although unimpressed by the kid's defiant tone, Belle let out an exasperated snort and pitched her card facedown onto the table.

"I thought you wanted it to be interesting," Clint chided.

Belle shook her head and waved off the comment. "Guess you could say I'm no longer interested."

That brought a laugh from three out of the five players. Niestrom merely shrugged and Tom was too focused to let himself show any emotion.

"That leaves you Allman," Clint announced.

The sergeant reached for his chips, but suddenly came to his senses and threw down his hold card. "Man needs to know his limits. I'm done."

Nodding, Clint looked back to Tom and pitched in his five dollars. Offhandedly, he snagged another stack and tossed it in. "Twenty-five again." When he saw that the kid was taking a moment to think, Clint added, "Put up or shut up. Isn't that the way?"

Seeing the casual look on Clint's face mixed in with everything else that was running through his own head, Tom gnashed his teeth and started to breathe heavily. His head twitched to one side so he could take a look at Niestrom. The gunfighter seemed to be waiting for this and when he saw Tom look, he nodded once.

"I . . . I'm sick of your lip, Adams," Tom snarled uncertainly. "And you can't talk to me like that."

"All I want is your decision, boy. Put up or shut up."

"Here's my decision." And with that, Tom stood up fast enough to send the chair flying backward behind him as his hand dropped for the gun at his side.

EIGHTEEN

Clint had seen this move coming from a mile away.

In fact, he'd been waiting for it to get here for the last two hours. After what Abby had said and after seeing how differently the kid had been acting after his talk with Niestrom, Clint figured that it was only a matter of time before Tom got up the nerve to make his play for glory.

By the time Tom was on his feet, Clint was already starting to move on his own. It was obvious by the intensity in his eyes that Tom was putting everything he had into this attack. But the truth of the matter was that he moved like molasses in the summertime compared to the way Clint's body reacted using nothing but reflex as his guide.

Another fact was that Tom's lack of speed was the main factor that kept him from choking on lead at that particular moment. Rather than pull his modified Colt just yet, Clint started to get up while reaching around behind him and grabbing hold of the back of his chair. As Tom was closing his fist around his pistol, Clint was straightening up and twisting his upper body in a way that lifted the chair up off the floor and got it moving.

Tom had the .44 out and pointed on target. His thumb

had the hammer pulled back halfway when Clint's chair swung around to catch him on the back of the legs. The thick pieces of wood slammed painfully against the nerve running from hip to knee, causing him to grunt loudly and skew to one side.

Following through with the rest of his momentum, Clint kept the blow going until the chair began to crack and snap under the impact. Tom wasn't solid enough to break the chair, however, and soon the makeshift club swept his boots right out from under him.

It looked as though the kid hung in midair for a second. By the time he'd realized what had happened, he was beginning to fall and when the full realization came, his ass was pounding solidly against the floor. Every bit of air inside his lungs rushed out in a loud grunt. When he tried to suck in another breath, all he could manage was a straining wheeze.

Everyone else at the table wasn't sitting idly by watching all of this. On the contrary, they burst out in a flurry of motion, each one of them going their own separate ways.

Not wanting anything to do with a barroom brawl, Sergeant Allman jumped to his feet and backed away. His hand rested on top of his service revolver, but stayed there. Sharp eyes darted back and forth beneath a furrowed brow, watching for the first sign of someone making a move toward either himself or his small pile of winnings.

Belle was grinning widely, an expression which looked bizarre on a face like hers. Her small, weathered hand was filled with a shiny pistol and she was stepping away from the table, preparing herself for whatever might be coming next. Already, her husband was moving in behind her, wielding a nasty blade in his leathery, dark-skinned hand.

Since he was anything but surprised by the actions of his pupil, Niestrom had already moved away from the table and was standing tall. He'd been able to clear leather, but wasn't able to get a clear shot since Clint had reacted in a way he hadn't quite foreseen.

Tom was sprawled out on the floor, his arms and legs flailing momentarily like a turtle which had been unceremoniously flipped onto its back. He regained his bearings much quicker than such an animal and was soon able to get his feet beneath him and get himself into a crouching position.

His lips curled back in an almost feral snarl, Tom shot up onto his feet and twisted his body into a classic sideways duelist's stance. His form was perfect. His aim wasn't even half bad, but he simply wasn't fast enough to take his shot before Clint managed to toss the table over using the toe of his boot.

Still holding on to the back of his chair, Clint swung his foot up in a forward arc, connecting with the table's edge. When the round slab of wood upended, it sent poker chips, cards and beer glasses spraying in Tom's direction, most of which were dumped onto the floor amid an earsplitting ruckus.

As soon as Clint saw that he'd managed to keep from separating the table from the piece in the middle which held it up, he dropped down to one knee and used it as a wooden shield. His hand went reflexively for the modified Colt at his side and his other hand pressed his hat tighter against his head as the air around him exploded with gunfire.

Having memorized the position of the others as well as the layout of the saloon, Clint knew the shots were coming from both Niestrom and Tom. The more he listened, however, the more convinced he became that there was a third party squeezing their trigger as well.

Lead tore through the air like a swarm of angry wasps, hissing over Clint's head and taking bites from the overturned table. Soon, the rounds started coming in at lower angles to punch holes through the tabletop that was Clint's only cover.

Clint knew it was only a matter of time before one of those bullets found its mark in his hide and so he made his move before that happened. Pushing off with his right leg, Clint emerged from behind the left side of the table, which put him almost immediately on top of Tom.

Charging in like an angry bull, Clint lowered his torso and slammed his shoulder against Tom's midsection. He could feel the solid impact through his upper body, but was stopped dead in his tracks once Tom braced himself with a quick repositioning of his feet.

By this time, the rest of the saloon was echoing with gunshots. Every once in a while, there was the crash of breaking glass or even the occasional rowdy holler, but all that concerned Clint at the moment was the sounds coming from the kid directly in front of him.

Blocking out everything else, Clint could hear Tom's labored breathing as well as the growl that welled up in the back of the kid's throat. But what he was waiting for was the distinctive metallic *click* of the hammer of Tom's .44 being snapped into position.

When that sound came, Clint's instincts kicked into action. It was either that, he knew, or die where he stood.

NINETEEN

Exploding with a sudden burst of motion, Clint took one step back with his left foot and then a step forward with his right. The movement launched his body into a quick spin that carried him off to the side and out of the path of Tom's gun just as the .44 went off.

The kid's expression was frozen like a photograph when the sparks roared from his barrel. Although there was a definite anticipation there, that was easily over-shadowed by a fright which burned all the way down to his soul. He'd wanted to pull that trigger, sure enough, but wasn't sure how to handle whatever was coming next.

But Clint couldn't see any of this. He might have figured it was there if he'd had much of a chance to figure out anything at all. For the time being, he was preoccupied with the task of staying alive.

He continued to spin until he'd rolled almost around to Tom's back. Once there, Clint pulled his left fist across his chest and jabbed it straight out again, digging his elbow into Tom's kidney. Even from where he was, Clint could hear the kid sucking in a painful breath and could see him bending forward in agony.

Luckily, Clint could also see Niestrom as he took careful aim and started to pull his trigger.

Niestrom's eyes narrowed as he watched Clint's every move. The instant Clint spotted him, the gunfighter took a quick shot and dove to one side. The bullet went high and wide, acting mainly as cover for his dive while Clint plucked the Colt from his holster.

Firing from the hip, Clint squeezed his own trigger and sent a round chasing at Niestrom's heels. But the other man had already dove for cover and the bullet burrowed harmlessly into a nearby wall.

Suddenly, there was a whole other set of shots coming from Clint's left side. When he took a quick look in that direction, he found Belle and Sam Starr mixing it up with a group of locals who'd been trying to scoop up the chips which had been scattered across the floor. Belle defended those chips as though they were her own life savings and Sam seemed only too happy to lend his knife to the cause.

One of those locals made the mistake of taking a shot at Belle and caught a bullet in the ribs for his trouble. When he didn't drop his gun right away, the poor sap also wound up with Sam's blade in his gut. The Cherokee snarled and stared the dying man in the eyes as he twisted the knife before tearing it out again.

Knowing that he had problems of his own at the moment, Clint turned his attention back to the pair of men intent on killing him just in time to see Tom wheeling around with fire in his eyes. Clint wanted to try and talk some sense into the kid, but knew he wouldn't get that chance if he allowed Tom to follow through on what he was about to do.

Gripping his gun in a trembling hand, Tom pulled back the hammer and quickly squeezed off a shot. Just as the gun went off, he felt a stinging pain in his wrist, which quickly turned into a wet heat.

The Colt in Clint's hand was smoking after having just

fired a round, which clipped Tom's wrist. The bullet's impact had been just enough to pull the kid's aim off target, and if it hadn't have been for Clint's modifications, the pistol wouldn't have been able to make the shot so quickly.

Clint flinched slightly as the lead from Tom's barrel whipped past his face. He knew what Tom was about to do as though he'd already seen it happen. It was called a border shift and was a maneuver normally used by shooters with two guns.

Rather than reload their pistol, many gunfighters carried another pistol that was already loaded. When they needed to trade one gun for another, they used a border shift to toss one gun into their other hand so they could draw their second weapon.

Although he didn't have another gun that anyone could see, Tom's hand was hurt and he still needed to fire. Sure enough, the kid went for the border shift, tossing the gun from his wounded hand into his left one. But Clint was ready for him and when the gun was in the air midway between Tom's hands, Clint reached out faster than a striking cobra and snatched the kid's pistol clean out of the air.

Tom's jaw dropped. If there weren't bullets still flying and blood still dripping onto the floorboards, the kid's expression might have even struck Clint as funny. But as it was, the furthest thing from Clint's mind was laughter.

"Think this over, kid," Clint said as he aimed one gun at him and the other at Niestrom. "I don't want to kill anyone." Even as he said that, Clint prepared himself to put a bullet through either man's skull.

After all, what a man wanted and what he had to do were oftentimes very different things.

TWENTY

All Clint had to do was look at Tom's face to know that the kid was having a moment of indecision. If Clint hadn't seen that same indecision all throughout the night, he wouldn't have even bothered trying to talk to him. Even with Tom's .44 in his possession, Clint was taking the biggest gamble of the entire night.

"You don't have anything to prove," Clint said. "And even if you did, you wouldn't prove a damn thing by dying here today."

Tom's eyes showed that he was thinking something over. Clint had no way of truly knowing what it was, but he figured that he must have hit a nerve if he'd managed to slow the kid down at all.

But even if Tom was trying to consider his options, it would have been awful hard to think about much of anything with all the other noise that was going on inside that saloon. All at once, the other shots and rowdy voices came rushing back over them, shattering whatever bit of concentration Tom had been able to manage.

Niestrom saw this just as well as Clint and took advantage of the distraction Tom was providing by making a play of his own. Waiting until Clint was looking more at

Tom than him, Niestrom took aim and pulled his trigger. He knew Clint would be firing as well and took a dive toward the floor, hoping he'd be quick enough to get out of the way of any return fire.

While Clint might have been feeling generous with the kid, those feelings did not extend to Niestrom. He'd figured the older gunfighter would pull something like this and had prepared himself accordingly. Clint fired the moment he saw movement coming from Niestrom and started to head for cover of his own.

Unfortunately, dividing his aim between two men cost Clint in the end. And it might have cost him dearly if Niestrom had taken his time with the one opening he managed to get.

Niestrom's bullet tore through the air amid a thunderous blast. The lead whipped toward Clint's skull and dug into flesh. A few inches was all it took to keep the round from being deadly to slicing deeply into Clint's cheek and hissing off toward the Yellow Dog's ceiling.

Clint's first shot punched through the middle of the space where Niestrom had been standing mere moments before diving for cover. The modified Colt barked again, this time punching a clean hole into Niestrom's leg and drilling all the way through to the other side.

Screeching in pain, Niestrom slipped and failed to catch himself with either hand and landed flat on his face. Half of his body wound up behind a table and the lower half was lying out in the open. Frantically, Niestrom used his hands to claw at the floor and pull himself completely behind the cover of tables and chairs.

Turning to the kid once again, Clint saw that Tom had made his decision and was grabbing for a holster which was strapped to his boot. His body reacted automatically, but just as Clint was about to defend himself, there came a piercing battle cry from another part of the saloon.

Both Tom and Clint turned to look. What they saw was

enough to send them both jumping away from each other as Sam Starr came charging toward them like a rampaging bull. The Cherokee now had a blade gripped in each hand, his arm pumping wildly in the air while his voice rattled throughout the room.

Clint dove back and landed on both feet, still ready for the kid to make his next move. Although he was fully prepared to return fire if Tom produced another gun, he wasn't about to blast the kid to hell unless it was absolutely necessary.

Since Tom seemed to have his hands full with the Indian as it was, Clint turned to try and find where Niestrom had gone. All he could see was the jumble of tables where the gunfighter had dived for cover. And the fact that he couldn't see Niestrom right away disturbed Clint more than if the gunfighter was on his feet and taking shots at him.

Just as he thought about that, Clint saw a flicker of movement from the corner of his eye. And just as he'd predicted, Clint saw Niestrom creeping up behind him with his gun drawn and ready to fire. The moment he was spotted, the gunfighter straightened up and plastered a defiant sneer onto his face.

"Now's the time, Adams," he said.

The rest of the noise inside the saloon seemed to die down for a moment or two, as if to give both men a chance to make their play. Clint knew that Niestrom was ready to draw, just as he knew that the kid would be watching his every move.

Niestrom squared off and stared down the bridge of his nose at the man who'd turned around to face him. The gunfighter's arm tensed as he spat, "Put up or shut up."

In reality, less than a second passed before Niestrom made his move. In Clint's mind, the span of time seemed to drag out a bit longer, simply because his senses were so busy soaking up every last detail they could find, from the way Niestrom stood, right down to the twitch in his mismatched eyes. All of it was important when it came to beating a man to the shot.

This time was no exception. Clint allowed Niestrom just enough slack to tip his hand before the modified Colt was readied, aimed and fired. The round Clint shot hissed through the air and punched Niestrom through the meat in his hip, spinning the gunfighter like a top and dropping him to the ground.

Knowing full well that Tom was still watching, Clint turned so he could make his final point to the boy.

"You see where—" Clint started to say.

But his words were cut off by a wild screaming and the pounding of rampaging feet. Emerging from behind Tom like a bad dream, Sam Starr thundered across the saloon with both blades swiping through the air. This time, however, the Cherokee was headed straight for Tom.

The kid's eyes went wide and all the emotion drained out of him. It was the very thing that Clint had been hoping not to see. For in that instant, as Tom swiveled and fired his gun at the frenzied Cherokee, he became the exact thing he'd been trying so hard to be.

His gun exploded only once.

That single bullet met Sam a second or two before the Indian could get close enough to bury those blades into the kid's flesh. And when the Indian dropped to both knees, he was sporting a gaping, bloody hole in the left side of his chest.

Clint watched the entire thing happen and as soon as he saw the round strike its target, he knew the fight was over. So rather than watch the rest of the grisly show, he ran across the room to kick Niestrom's gun away from the gunfighter's reach.

"Sam!" came the rough voice which was hoarse from so much screaming and carrying on. "Oh dear lord, Sam!"

By the time Belle got to the Cherokee's side, her husband was already nothing more than a crumpled, dead shell. She dropped down to her knees and held him in her arms, crying over him as though he'd just been some innocent bystander cut down in the prime of his life.

Although Clint didn't hold any grudges against Sam Starr, it was hard to feel sorry for him after seeing the way he'd chosen to spend the last moments of his life. As much as he hated to see the gleeful smile spread over Tom's face, Clint knew that the Indian had gotten what was rightfully his.

"I did it!" Tom exclaimed. Looking around, he saw all the amazed looks directed at him from just about everyone inside the saloon. Even Sergeant Allman seemed vaguely impressed. "I did it!"

"Yeah, kid," Clint said under his breath. "You sure did."

TWENTY-ONE

The sheriff put in an appearance, but didn't have much to do besides step over the bigger messes and have a talk with Dave. Although the barkeep had suffered a few broken glasses and some damaged furniture, he actually seemed pleased as punch to have such a first-rate brawl in his establishment.

The way he saw it, the Yellow Dog would only benefit from the fight once word about it spread. And having the law come in to arrest anyone involved with such an event would just be a crying shame. Since the sheriff hadn't been expecting anything less, he walked straight over to the single dead body resulting from the ruckus and had a look for himself.

"That's Sam Starr?" the lawman asked.

Belle was still standing over the body. "That's my husband," she said. "And the man that done this is gonna pay with his own blood."

The lawman shifted on his feet, but otherwise looked none too worked up about any of what he'd seen. "Who might that man be?"

"I'll worry about that," she replied, looking pointedly

over to where Tom was standing at the bar. "Where's my gun?"

After squatting down next to the dead Cherokee, the sheriff scratched absently at his bushy mustache and then straightened back up again. He plucked a small pistol from where it had been wedged in his gun belt and said, "This the gun you're talking about?"

Belle made a grab for the weapon, but wasn't fast enough to snatch it from the lawman's hand before it closed and moved out of her reach.

"I'll take that as a yes," he said. "Dave handed it over. Frankly, I'm impressed he managed to get his hands on it."

"Must've slipped out've my hand when I saw what happened to my Sam."

"Well, it stays with me all the same. The way I see it, you'd only cause me a headache if I let you have a gun right this instant."

Turning on the sheriff like a wolf that was about to lunge for a bared throat, Belle took a step forward and brought herself up close to the lawman. "My husband's dead and that's how you treat me? What kind of shameful law are you?"

"I'm the kind that knows who you are, Mrs. Starr. And I'm also the kind that could very well take you in and get myself a nice reward from one of those people you stole from over the years."

"I served my time," she snarled.

"Good for you. Now why don't you take a little time to mourn and thank your good fortune that I'm being so generous to a recently widowed . . . lady . . . such as yourself." The voice he used when he said "lady" sounded every bit as convincing as a preacher making excuses for a couple living in sin.

But while Belle didn't seem at all happy with the way things turned out, she had seen enough lawmen in her

time to appreciate being able to walk away from such a
meeting with her freedom in tact. Turning her back on
the sheriff in an exaggerated huff, she stepped over to her
husband's body and started whispering quietly into the
dead man's ear.

"Looks like a messy case of self-defense," the lawman
said. "Anyone wants to file a complaint, they know where
they can find me." And with a tip of his hat, he said his
good-byes to Dave and the familiar faces that had remained inside the saloon before walking out through the
front door. On his way back to his office, the lawman
found himself surprised that the Yellow Dog wasn't more
filled with curious bystanders. After all, that was what the
place was famous for and that was why he'd let the fight
pass by so lightly. It wouldn't do to put a black mark on
such a profitable business.

Saloons paid taxes too. And saloon keepers like Dave
were powerful members of the Clark community. In fact,
the sheriff thought he might just have secured himself
another appointment once election time rolled by again.

Stepping down off the boardwalk, the lawman passed
one of the other participants in the brawl and since he
didn't feel like reopening that can of worms, he simply
tipped his hat to the gunman and continued on his way.

"What's he look so happy about?" Clint asked when he
saw the sheriff walk by.

Abby had come out to stand next to him on the boardwalk. Both of them were taking in the fresh air, clearing
the smell of stale gunpowder and cigar smoke from their
lungs.

In response to Clint's question, she smiled and said,
"You'd be pretty happy too if you had a job like his without having to do much of anything to keep it. Actually,
the less he does, the longer he'll stay sheriff."

"I guess there wasn't much for him to do, anyway."

"Locking up Tom Bolander would have been good enough for me."

Clint looked over to Abby and the first thing he noticed was the way she clasped her arms around herself as though she was trying to fight back a chill. The air was cool, but the wind was calm and fairly temperate for this time of year. "He really bothers you, doesn't he?"

"Yes," she said in a distracted voice. "He really does." After mulling something over in her head, she let out a breath and turned to face Clint head-on. "But not anymore."

"That's funny," Clint said. "Because he only just started bothering me."

Abby seemed confused by this for a moment, but then she saw something that expelled the questions right from her mind. The Yellow Dog's front door swung open and someone came outside with steps so heavy that they shook Abby where she stood.

It was Tom. Judging by the way he moved, one might have thought that he'd grown a foot or two since the last time he'd passed through that same door. When he saw Abby, he set his eyes on her like a wolf picking out the slowest deer in the field. A smile slid onto his lips, his eyes flicked with a wink and he moved on. When he saw Clint, the smile stayed, but took a somewhat darker hue.

Clint returned the stare with one of his own, causing the kid to look away in less than a second.

Niestrom emerged from the saloon a second or two later. His limp contorted every step and forced him to move like a broken puppet, but he still couldn't have looked any happier. Walking past Abby, the gunfighter positioned himself directly in front of Clint. His gray eye seemed especially bright, but the white one looked as though it had been filled with curdled milk. "I've got to say I'm surprised at you, Adams."

Clint allowed himself a slight grin and his eyes dropped

down to the bloody wound in the other man's leg. "Me too. I'm surprised you managed to get up off the floor and walk out of there like a man. Well . . . something like a man."

Chuckling under his breath, Niestrom tried to keep up appearances. Clint wasn't fooled, however, since he wasn't concerned with the way the gunfighter was acting. Just like when they were playing cards not too long ago, Clint could see right through the gunfighter as if Niestrom were made from dirty glass.

"You made a mistake tonight, Adams," Niestrom said. "You should've finished me off when you had the chance."

Clint remained silent, channeling his intensity through his eyes, which burned into the gunfighter. It took only slightly longer to turn Niestrom away than it did his protegee.

"You're gonna be sorry you let me live," Niestrom said even as he was moving away like a scolded dog. "But you'll be even more sorry you let Tommy Bolander go. He's the devil himself." Turning toward the Yellow Dog, Niestrom shouted, "Tommy Bolander. The devil himself!"

TWENTY-TWO

Abby watched as Niestrom hobbled down from the board-walk and stepped onto the street. Tom was waiting for him, gazing up defiantly at Adams as though he'd just decided that he'd found his newest, worst enemy. "Is he crazy?" she asked quietly.

If Clint heard the question, he didn't give the slightest indication. Instead, he was staring right back at Tom in a way that had a definite effect on the younger man. Clint's eyes were burning slits and the power in them was so intense that it was almost like heat rising up from a baking desert floor.

Just like all the other times he'd tried, Tom was unable to keep his eyes focused on Clint for more than a couple seconds. When Niestrom came up and started whispering something to him, the kid blinked and turned away. Tom looked back once more, only to find Clint glaring back at him in the exact way he'd left him.

Abby looked from one man to another, glancing from Clint to Tom and back again. While she could tell that something was going on that she wasn't quite aware of, she was too tired to try and figure it out. "Is he—" she started to say.

"No," Clint interrupted. "He's not crazy. He's just trying to prove his point."

"And did he?"

Looking over his shoulder, Clint nodded toward the door to the Yellow Dog which stood open to reveal the commotion that was once again brewing inside the saloon. "See for yourself."

Dave and the rest of his workers were scrambling about the place, trying to clean up. A few people were tending to people's wounds. And everyone else couldn't stop talking excitedly about what had happened and comparing notes on what they'd seen.

"I guess he did," Abby said. Reaching out with one hand, she took hold of the edge of the door and pushed it shut. As soon as the Yellow Dog was closed up again, the world around them seemed to calm back down to its normal pace. "That's better."

Even Clint felt as though he could breathe easier. "It certainly is."

"So what was the deal with that staring contest between you and Tom?"

Shaking his head, Clint let out a weary breath. "Just two dogs circling each other."

"Trying to stake out your places in the same yard?"

"Something like that," Clint said with a grin. "I wonder if I was ever like that?"

Abby got real close to him and slipped her arms around his waist. The heat from her body soaked through Clint's clothes to warm him all the way down to his bones. "I haven't known you that long," she said softly. "But I have a hard time imagining you as *anything* like that."

"I don't."

Her eyes wrinkled as her face reflected a subtle mix of shock and confusion. "Really?"

Clint nodded. "I've never been out to impress anyone by chalking up killings to my name or trying to scare other folks, but on some level, any man who takes up a gun is like Tom. It's a necessity, really. There's a way you have to carry yourself, a way you have to talk and a way you have to walk."

"It seems complicated."

"It sure does when you think about it, but it's not. It feels more like instinct. You don't work at looking for all the little signs that you get. They just come to you." Clint paused for a second and mulled that over. "You just know when someone's got their eye on you or if they're about to make a move in the wrong direction. That's what keeps you alive."

"So you can tell all that just by looking at someone?" Abby asked.

"There's a bit more to it than that, but . . . yeah," Clint said as though he was almost surprised to hear himself say it. "It's just a kind of sense you pick up after a while. I'm sure you have your own kind of sense and you don't even know it."

"Oh, I know it well enough, Clint Adams," Abby said. When she spoke, her entire bearing shifted in a way that made him feel like something was pulling him closer to her. Abby's hips shifted slightly and her voice became softer, more playful. "I may not have taken up a gun, but I can tell a whole lot about a man just by looking at him. That's the way *I* make a living."

Looking at her, Clint felt the rest of the world melting away and that nothing else really mattered except for him and Abby. "That sounds suspicious to me," he chided.

Abby played along with it perfectly. She moved her hands up over his chest and looked at him with a playful twinkle in her eye. "Suspicious? Not at all." She lowered her eyes for a moment and when she brought them up again, she gave him a wry smirk. "Well . . . maybe a little."

Clint straightened up and took a step back. Crossing his

arms, he said, "All right, then. What can you tell about me?"

Rubbing her chin and looking him up and down, she thought for a moment and then nodded. "I can see you're angry that your poker game got cut short and you wish Third Eye Niestrom would dry up and blow away."

"Damn, you're good."

"And I can also see that you're worried about Tom," she said in a more serious tone. "You think that he might still be able to turn around and have a good, long life if only he'd forget about trying to get himself killed."

Nodding, Clint said, "Now that really was good. How did you know that?"

"Because anyone else would have killed Tom back in that saloon and they would have been right to do it. A blind man could see you wanted that boy to live. Lord knows why, but you did." Once those words had hung in the air between them for a couple seconds, Abby lightened her features again and said, "You know what else I can tell?"

"What?"

"That you want to come with me and catch up on some old times. That you want to be with me all night long so we can forget about everything else for a while and enjoy every last second until we fall over from exhaustion."

Clint shook his head slowly. "Now *that* was just plain impressive."

TWENTY-THREE

Abby took Clint by the hand and started leading him away from the Yellow Dog. Every couple steps or so, she would look over her shoulder and smile in a way that let him know she was looking forward to their night together every bit as much as he was. They were just about to turn the corner when suddenly a voice came chasing after them.

"Mister Adams! Mister Adams!"

Stopping for a second without looking back, Clint acted as though he hadn't heard anything but the rush of the wind and their feet grinding against the dirt.

"Mister Adams! Clint!"

Clint was set to keep ignoring the voice until something about it struck a chord in the back of his mind. It didn't take long for him to make a connection and when he did, he stopped one more time. "Sandra?" he said to himself while looking over his shoulder.

Abby pulled at him insistently. "Forget about whoever that is and come with me," she urged. "I don't want to think about that place anymore tonight."

Sure enough, when Clint looked to see who was calling his name, he immediately spotted the waitress who he'd

93

been talking to at Mil's Place. "Jesus, I completely forgot," he whispered as the blonde came rushing over to him and Abby.

"Why is that woman chasing after you?" Abby asked.

"I talked to her earlier tonight and she—"

"Is that Sandra Lockings from Mil's Place?"

"Yes it is and I was—"

"She looks awful glad to see you," Abby said in a way that made it obvious she had a pretty good idea about what was going on. "Should I be jealous here?"

The blonde was almost up to them and had slowed her pace now that she saw Clint was willing to wait for her. As she got closer, Clint turned around and Abby moved in behind him.

"I invited Sandra to meet me at the Yellow Dog," he said. "We were talking at dinner and she seemed nice enough."

"You don't have to explain to me, Clint Adams," Abby whispered. "Just be sure to hurry up and get to the hotel right down the street over there. Room number five. If you keep me waiting too long, I'll have to punish you."

"And if I can't get away soon enough, I'll—"

Abby put her mouth directly onto Clint's ear. When she spoke, her soft lips fluttered against him like butterfly wings. "You can bring her along."

Whatever Clint was about to say was instantly forgotten. He could hear Abby walking away and could see Sandra approaching, but all he could think about was the world of possibility that Abby had just brought to mind. What made it even more maddening was that he was fairly certain that she wasn't kidding.

Sandra stepped up to him and gave him a quick peck on the cheek. "There you are, Clint. I almost thought I'd lost you in all the commotion back there." Looking at him in amusement, Sandra wrinkled her nose and laughed once. "What's the matter, Clint? You look all flustered."

Clint was able to pull his mind back into the present and focused in on what he was doing. "Yeah, well, you know . . . all the commotion." With that reminding him, Clint took a closer look at Sandra. "How much did you see?"

Her eyes widened somewhat and some color flushed through her cheeks. "I saw everything. In fact, I'd just seen you at the table playing cards when it all started."

"Are you all right? Did you get hurt?"

Sandra waved off Clint's concerns immediately. "Oh I'm fine. All I saw was someone swinging a chair and the table went over and then everything else became a blur. One of Dave's boys pulled me behind the bar and that's when the shooting started.

"I tried to get a look at what was going on, but there was so much happening and so many people about. Did you know that some of those other card players were starting fights on their own? I think they were trying to grab the money from the tables while the rest of the players were watching the fight."

Clint listened to Sandra expounding the finer points of the exchange and couldn't help but be drawn in by her words. Although he was in the middle of the entire thing, it was interesting to hear about it from another point of view. The more he heard from the blonde, the more Clint had to agree with her.

It *was* exciting. At least, from her point of view.

"What about you?" she asked once she'd brought him up to speed on her story. "Did you get hurt?"

"I got bumped around a bit, but it's nothing I'm not used to."

Sandra went from excited to concerned in the blink of an eye. She rushed forward and fretted with his collar and face, searching for anything that looked remotely like a wound. "Oh my goodness, what happened?"

"That wasn't a stage show you were watching in there,

Sandra. Those were real bullets flying in there."

"I know. I didn't mean that . . ." Sandra let her explanation trail off the moment she realized that she wouldn't be able to say exactly the right thing. So rather than try to talk anymore, she moved her face in closer and let her actions speak for her.

Her lips were thinner than Abby's, but the feeling behind them was much more intense. And when she didn't feel any resistance from Clint, she pressed in even closer, her tongue slipping easily into his mouth.

They kissed there for several minutes. Neither one of them wanted to break away and soon their hands were roaming freely over the other's body. Sandra's hair smelled like springtime flowers and she tasted vaguely of honey. The more Clint thought about those things, the more the rest of his body sought to taste more of her.

Sandra reacted to this at first by moaning quietly. Then, as she started rubbing against him and chewing on his bottom lip with growing passion, she suddenly stepped back. Her lips were the last things to break contact and when they did, she ran her tongue over them as if to soak up the last bit of him that she could taste.

"I didn't mean for that to happen," she said. Judging by the tone in her voice, she was telling him the god's honest truth.

Clint's heart was pounding in his chest and his lungs strained to pull in more of the air which carried her scent. "It's all right. Sometimes these things happen."

"They usually don't happen to me," she said. "But after all the excitement, I feel like my heart's racing a mile a minute and I can't catch my breath."

"I know the feeling."

Regaining her normal senses, Sandra lowered her eyes and took another step back. "I just wanted to see if you were all right. Maybe . . . I think I should go."

Clint could tell that the blonde wanted nothing more

than for him to stop her. Even a word in that direction would have been enough, but no matter how nice of a surprise her attention had been, his thoughts were already drifting back to the brunette waiting for him in a nearby room.

"Thanks for checking on me," Clint said.

The disappointment was on her face, but there was also something else that connected them once again, even though they were no longer touching. "Maybe some other time," she said while turning to walk away.

By the tone in her voice and the wriggle in her stride, Clint knew that those last words weren't meant as a farewell, but as a promise. For the moment, however, he had his own appointment to keep.

TWENTY-FOUR

Less than three streets away from the Yellow Dog, all that could be heard was the distant echo of voices coming from the saloon as well as the occasional rattle of the wind bouncing off of windows. That somewhat peaceful silence was shattered by the literally gut-wrenching sound of someone spilling their last meal onto the dirt in a messy heap.

After pulling in a few desperate breaths, the man kneeling in a narrow alleyway arched his back again and spewed up another batch. Another man stood behind him, patting the first figure on the back with one hand while tipping a flask to his lips with the other.

"That's all right," Niestrom said without even trying to sound convincing in his sentiment. "Go on and get it all out. You'll feel a helluva lot better."

Below, the gunfighter Tom Bolander started to lift himself up off the ground, but immediately dropped down again as his body went through yet another set of convulsions. Unable to vomit even if he'd wanted to, Tom spat twice into the dirt and stood up.

"Here," Niestrom said while handing over a handkerchief he'd pulled from his jacket pocket. "Use this."

The kid swiped his mouth and handed the handkerchief back. "Thanks, John."

Eyeing the handkerchief as though that was somehow more disgusting than everything else he'd just been forced to watch, Niestrom crumpled up the square of material and tossed it to the ground. "Don't mention it. You feeling better?"

Tom filled his lungs with clean air and let it out. "That was Clint Adams back there. Holy shit, I just drew down on Clint Adams and I'm still here."

"Damn right you're still here. You did real good. Not great, but real damn good. By the way . . . what happened to that ace in the hole you were so proud of?"

"Huh? Oh . . . she was there. She just must've hid somewhere when the shooting started. But I know she would've stayed to watch. She likes that sort of thing."

"Oh does she? And what was she supposed to do for you tonight?"

"She'll be there when I need her," Tom said confidently. "You'll see."

The longer he went over what had gone on that night, the more Tom couldn't believe it. After thinking through it a few more times, he not only started to believe it, but he also started to feel what it would be like to be a true gunman.

A bad man.

Someone the normal folks feared and respected. The type of man they wrote books about years after they'd died.

Suddenly, Tom's face twitched and he looked over to Niestrom. "What do you mean it wasn't great?"

Niestrom smirked in a way that looked as humorous as a shotgun in the mouth. "I mean just what I said. Adams could've killed you any time he saw fit and if you don't know that, then you're a hell of a lot dumber than I ever thought."

For a moment, Tom looked about ready to bust. Then he felt another kick in his stomach to remind him of what had really gone on earlier that night. "He could've killed me."

"Yep."

Thinking about what had happened at the Yellow Dog, Tom stared into space, flinching whenever the sound of gunfire echoed through his memories. "Jesus Christ." Looking down at his wounded hand as though he needed verification, Tom stared at the dried blood which had already soaked through the bandage wrapped over his palm. "He could've killed me."

"But you know what the most important part was?" Niestrom asked. "He didn't."

Tom swallowed hard and nodded. The movement was so weak, it looked as though it might have been caused by the wind. His eyes were more focused, however, and his breathing was slowing to a more normal pace.

Niestrom reached out and chucked the kid on the shoulder like some kind of proud sibling. "You called out the Gunsmith himself and took a scratch for your troubles. Do you know how many others have wound up buried six feet under for doing that same thing?"

Tom started to reply, but turned pale and started to wobble uncertainly before he could get his mouth to form the words.

Resting his hand on Tom's shoulder to hold the younger man steady, Niestrom answered his own question with, "More than I can count, that's how many. But you're not one of 'em. And no matter what else you could've done, that's the most important thing. You're not one of those shit heels to catch a bullet. You said your piece and god be damned about the consequences."

After taking another pull from his flask, Niestrom offered it to the kid who all but ripped it from his hand. "And that's why I wanted you to do that back there," the gunfighter said. "It was time for you to show the world what you're made of."

"But . . . there was only—"

"It don't matter how many folks were in that saloon," Niestrom interrupted. "Because the folks that go to the Yellow Dog go to catch a look at famous men. Bad men. They go there to see things they'll remember and when they go to some other saloon in some other part of the state, they'll talk about what they saw.

"They'll be talking about what happened here tonight. They'll spread the word and they'll remember your name. That's why you've got to take on men like Adams. You've got to build a name for yourself because once you do, men like him will step aside when they see you coming."

Although still a little green around the edges, Tom was starting to get his bearings back once again. The kid's insides had been doing everything from spinning excitedly inside of him to dropping to the bottom of his boots.

One moment, he'd be ready to take on the world, and the next he wanted only to hide from it. What shook him the most was the fact that he'd never been closer to dying than he had less than an hour ago. Staring into Clint Adams's eyes, Tom swore he could feel the reaper tapping him on the shoulder. And now that it was over . . .

"How do you feel?" Niestrom asked.

"Fine. I feel fine."

"Good, because now that this town knows you're truly a bad man, they need to know you can finish what you started. The next time we see Adams, only one of you will walk away."

TWENTY-FIVE

Every step Clint took toward the hotel where Abby was waiting, it felt as though he was taking ten steps away from the Yellow Dog Saloon. All the sounds of people telling and retelling the night's events still drifted through the air nearly half a block away. The noise only grew louder as people began stumbling out of the saloon in groups, still swapping tidbits regarding the barroom fight.

Clint shook his head and kept walking toward the hotel. He knew well enough that people would gossip no matter what. If it wasn't about him, it would just be about someone else. The gossip itself hadn't gotten to him in a long time. It was the noise of it that was starting to get on his nerves.

After spending an entire night in a crowded saloon, Clint's ears were jangling like bells attached to the sides of his head. Of course, the gunshots hadn't done wonders to help that situation, but they made him all the more anxious to find some way of soothing his nerves. To this end, he headed toward Abby's hotel, taking his time and soaking up the relative quiet of the night.

He got to the front of the building and looked up at the windows. Most of them were dark, but one or two were flickering with a weak light coming from within. There was some movement at one of the dark windows and when Clint turned his attention toward that one, he saw the curtains move away and someone step up to look outside.

At first, all Clint could see was the vague outline of a person standing there. But when he took a moment to look a little harder, he saw that it was Abby looking down at him. It was still a bit dark for Clint to make out details, but he could recognize the way her hair fell over her face and clung to the base of her neck.

Spotting him, Abby pulled the curtains aside even more so that Clint could see her all the way down to just past her waist. It seemed as though she was luminescent in the shadows, but that was only partly due to her smooth, pale skin. She was also wearing a white lace bustier which hugged the curves of her body and cupped her breasts perfectly.

She stood in the window with her arms outstretched, holding the curtains open for him to see. Cocking her hips to one side, Abby smiled down at him and slowly turned, displaying herself to him proudly.

Clint had stopped moving. He felt rooted to the spot as he watched her sexy little show, drinking in the sight of her as she completed her turn. Even though he was still down on the street, his eyes were working doubly hard to take in as much of her as was humanly possible. The mixture of dim moonlight and hazy shadows only helped to accentuate her curves, making it possible for him to run his gaze over her round breasts, the curve of her spine, as well as the firm upper slope of her buttocks.

When she completed her little presentation and turned around to face him again, Abby looked surprised to see Clint still standing there in the dark looking up at her. In fact, the instant Clint thought of that, he was surprised at himself for the same reason.

The remedy for that situation was simple enough. Although it was hard for him to purposely look away from the window, it only made him move that much faster as he all but jumped onto the boardwalk and charged into the hotel. The last thing Clint saw before losing sight of Abby was her smiling widely, obviously appreciating the effect she'd had upon him.

Clint pushed the front door open and was about to bound up the stairs when he saw that he'd attracted the attention of a spindly man sitting behind the front desk. He studied Clint over a folded newspaper, his eyes magnified significantly through a pair of thick spectacles.

"I'm just going to see Abby Tyler," Clint said with one foot on the bottom step of a narrow staircase and one hand upon the banister.

Despite the fact that he was looking straight at him, the old man behind the desk still hadn't moved. In fact, for a second or two, Clint wondered if the guy wasn't sleeping with his eyes open. Finally, the old clerk spoke, but the movement of his lips was covered by the newspaper. "Isn't it a bit late for that?" he asked.

Trying to look past how disconcerting it was to speak to a living statue, Clint put on his friendliest smile and climbed up another step. "I know, but she's expecting me. We'll try to . . ." Clint stopped himself in midsentence when he reminded himself that he wasn't some boy sneaking into a girl's bedroom and the man behind the desk wasn't Abby's patron.

"We'll try to be quiet," he said with finality and climbed the stairs two at a time.

Once he was at the top of the staircase, Clint looked down the proper side of the hall to where Abby's room should be. Although he had a fairly good idea, judging from where her window was, he didn't need to look that hard since she stood waiting for him in her doorway with one foot rubbing up and down along the frame.

"Took you long enough," she said in a soft, sensuous voice.

Clint walked straight up to her and slid his hands around her body, pulling her close to him. His lips found hers and when he kissed her, Clint could feel Abby writhing against him as though she'd been just as anxious for this moment to arrive as he was.

Letting his hands roam over her hips and down to her thighs, Clint slipped his tongue into her mouth and pressed her up against the door. He only broke the kiss for a second, but quickly tasted her again as he started nibbling along the side of her neck. Clint's hands moved down to cup her firm backside. The instant Abby felt this, she hopped up and wrapped her legs around his waist, grabbing him tightly with both arms around his neck and shoulders.

Acting on impulse, Abby reached down between her legs and started pulling open Clint's pants. She was able to reach inside and stroke him before they could both hear footsteps coming from the bottom of the stairs.

Hearing that was the only thing to make Clint stop kissing Abby's fragrant skin. He moved away from the door, carrying Abby with him and stepped into her room. She was breathing heavily, her eyes filled with excitement as she reached out to push the door shut. The slamming sound still echoed through the room as Clint pressed Abby against the wall next to the frame and picked up right where he'd left off.

TWENTY-SIX

The bed seemed too far away for Clint to carry her there just yet. All he wanted to do was caress her body and feel the heat as it came off her skin and soaked directly into his. Her breath rushed over his neck and breezed into his ear, mixed with the occasional satisfied groan or whispering of his name.

Clint's fingers slipped beneath the filmy material of her lingerie and found her flesh hot and soft to the touch. Cupping her bottom, Clint squeezed gently and pressed himself against her, bringing another excited groan from the back of Abby's throat.

Leaning back to allow Abby's hands free access over him, Clint felt the torture of putting his desires on hold. That torture paid off instantly, however, as Abby freed his cock from his pants and slid her hands up and down along its length. Clint could feel himself getting harder with every stroke of her hands and before too long, he was leaning in and whispering into her ear.

"Put me inside you," he said while using one hand to pull her panties aside. "I want you right now."

Abby drew in a sharp breath. The beating of her heart caused her breasts to tremble as she leaned back against the wall and spread her legs a little wider. Squirming within Clint's strong grasp, she shifted her hips until the top of his penis rubbed against the pink, wet lips of her vagina. She drew in a sharper breath when she fit him between those lips, letting it out as he slid all the way inside.

Starting slowly at first, Clint pumped his hips back and forth, savoring the way Abby's body wrapped around his in a slick, warm embrace. She fit tightly around him and when he thrust into her as deeply as he could, Abby's muscles tensed just enough to massage his cock as he pulled out once again.

Abby had opened her eyes by this point and was staring straight at Clint as he worked between her legs. She could feel the motion of his body as he worked to thrust in and out of her. The muscles in his arms and shoulders felt wonderful beneath her fingers and around her body. All it took was a simple shift of her lower body to position herself so that his shaft rubbed against her clit with every stroke.

Now the pleasure was pulsing through them both at such a rate that Clint and Abby lost themselves completely to the moment. Their bodies moved as one in a rhythm that grew quicker and more intense as every second passed.

Abby felt as if she were floating through the air as she let her head loll backward and surrender herself to Clint's arms. Her body moved on its own accord, hips pumping with his and legs pulling him in tight.

When Abby opened her eyes, she realized that she actually had been moving. Clint had carried her away from the wall and was walking toward the bed.

His arms wrapped tightly around her, Clint was about to set Abby down when he stopped and stayed right where he was. Although he'd broken their rhythm by moving toward the bed, she was still grinding up and down against him, riding his cock and tossing her head from side to side.

Watching her was almost enough to drive him close to the edge, but the sensations she was giving him were more than enough to push him over it. It took everything he had to keep from letting the pleasure overwhelm him, but Clint managed to hold back before it was too late.

He waited for her to thrust against him and then held her body in that position. Even the way she wriggled there sent chills through his flesh. When Abby locked her eyes on to him, she opened her mouth and licked her lips invitingly.

"Had enough already?" she asked playfully.

Clint smiled and set her down on the mattress. "Not hardly." And without another word, he crawled onto the bed and pushed open her legs, kneeling there as she propped herself up on her elbows.

Her eyes wandered over his body, lingering on his rigid penis and staring at it longingly. Abby's face took on a smoldering heat and she reached up to run her fingers over her breasts as though she couldn't go another moment without intimate contact.

Clint had been about to enter her again, but found that he wanted to watch what she was doing for a little bit. Just to see how she would react, Clint brushed his fingers along the moist lips between her legs, allowing his thumb to graze the swollen nub of her clitoris.

Smiling at first, Abby soon clenched her eyes shut and leaned her head back as an orgasm suddenly swept through her body. The climax was so intense that she could only grit her teeth and allow it to wash over her entire body.

Reading the expression on her face as well as the motion of her hips, Clint knew just when to keep his fingers moving and exactly when to leave them right where they were. Watching her as she climaxed was almost as good as being inside of her. The sound of her panting and the feel of her skin as she wantonly rubbed up against him made Clint want to prolong the moment for as long as he could.

But she could only stand so much and when the tingling beneath Abby's flesh subsided, she opened her eyes and laid her back flat against the bed. For the next couple of moments, she moved her hands over her body, gently touching her stomach, rubbing her nipples and slipping her fingers between her legs. All the while, she never took her eyes away from Clint. In fact, Abby was thoroughly enjoying the expressions that drifted across his face while watching her.

"You like watching me, don't you?" Abby whispered.

"You know I do. But I'd like something else even more."

And before Abby could say another word, her breath was taken away by the feeling of Clint's fingers moving aside and his cock sliding once again inside of her. She clutched the sheets with both hands and moaned softly as he drove deeply between her thighs.

Clint took hold of Abby's legs and set her ankles upon his shoulders. From there, he pumped in and out until his moans were mingling with hers in the dark.

TWENTY-SEVEN

The sun was beaming through the window of Abby's room by the time she and Clint were ready to move again. They'd spent the previous night and a good part of that morning alternating between sleep and sex. One would lead to another as they followed their natural whims whenever they felt compelled to do so.

One round of intense lovemaking would lead to an hour or so of sleep and when they had gathered some strength, their bodies would once again be entwined. Spent that way, the hours flowed by easily and night quickly brightened into day.

Clint swung his feet over the side of the bed, stretching cramped muscles and shielding his eyes from the brilliant sunlight. "What time is it?" he wondered out loud.

"Not time to leave," Abby replied in a sexy pout. She moved up behind Clint and slid her arms around him from behind, massaging his chest with both hands. "I want you to stay here for a while."

Scooting up to the edge of the mattress, Clint reached out for his clothes and said, "I can't stay here."

Abby let him move out from her arms and sat up on the bed. "Why not? Are you headed out of town again

110

after having your fun or are you thinking about Tom and Niestrom?"

"Neither. I'm starving. Spending the night with you works up one hell of an appetite."

Lightening up a bit, Abby smiled and leaned against the headboard. She allowed the sheet to fall away from her naked body and shifted so that she was lying on her side. "The hotel serves lunch downstairs, but I'm here right now. I can think of a way to pass the time until the meal is served."

Clint was hiking up his pants and reaching for his shirt as he looked at Abby. "I'll bet you can. But if I don't get out of here soon, I may never want to leave."

"Would that be so bad?" she asked while crawling across the mattress and reaching out for Clint's belt buckle.

If Clint had a good reason for getting dressed and leaving that room, it flew right out of his head when Abby pulled his pants down past his knees and reached out to cup him. His body reacted instantly to her touch and before Abby had closed her lips around the tip of his cock, he was fully erect and unable to even consider walking away.

Her lips were soft and full, moving up and down along the length of his penis in slow, easy strokes. Before too long, her tongue was caressing him as well, sending waves of pleasure down through his legs and up along his spine.

Clint slipped his fingers through Abby's thick black hair, holding the back of her head as she bobbed back and forth. Before he had a chance to catch his breath, he was fully undressed and lying on the bed, Abby on top, straddling him.

Smiling triumphantly, Abby leaned forward and kissed Clint on the mouth as her hips pumped slowly up and down. "There now," she whispered. "Is this so bad?"

For a moment, all Clint could do was return Abby's kiss and run his hands over the sumptuous curve of her buttocks. That was more than enough to answer her question and they spent the next half hour without another word passing between them.

The only sound in the room was their steady, intense breathing as Clint and Abby worked their appetite to new heights.

They emerged from Abby's room hand in hand. She straightened the folds of her skirts while looking up at Clint with a devilish grin.

"I think I'm ready for some food right about now," she teased. "Thanks to you, I'm almost ready to fall over."

"Well, thanks to you I'm not able to walk straight."

Clint was amused to see that, despite all the things they'd done over the last twelve hours, he was still able to make Abby blush.

Lowering her head and suppressing a naughty laugh, she walked down ahead of him and all but rushed through the front door. When Clint stepped into the lobby, the first thing he noticed was that the same old man was sitting behind the front desk.

Not only that, but he was sitting in the same position and wearing the same crusty look upon his sour face. The only thing that had changed about him was the clothes on his back and the edition of the newspaper in his hand.

Clint waved to the old-timer and said, "Good morning to you."

The old man followed Clint with his eyes and grunted a reply.

Just as Clint was about to turn toward the door and walk outside, his eyes caught on the headline of the morning paper and stayed there. His feet stopped moving and his hand froze on the handle of the door.

"What is it, Clint?" Abby asked, the smile on her face

dropping away once she'd noticed the way Clint was standing. "What's wrong?"

Letting out an exasperated sigh, Clint walked toward the front desk and squinted to try and read the upside-down headline. The old-timer kept his issue folded in hand, but pointed to a stack of papers in the corner of the room.

"You can pay for yer own, mister," he croaked. "I suppose you'll be wanting to buy more'n one."

Flipping a coin onto the desk, Clint went to where the papers had been dropped and took one from the top of the stack. He stood near the doorway and held the paper out in both hands so he could get a look at the headline.

GUNFIGHT AT THE YELLOW DOG

In smaller letters beneath that, the copy read, "Clint Adams called out by gunfighter Tom Beaulander and John 'Third Eye' Niestrom." The copy went on to give a colorful rendition of the fight from the night before and concluded with the notation that both men were "cowed" by Clint's prowess and escaped into the night.

Abby came up behind Clint and put a hand on his shoulder. "What's the matter Clint?" she asked again while trying to get a look at the paper in his hands. Once she got a chance to read through a bit of the article, she looked back to Clint and said, "Maybe now Tom will be satisfied. This is probably just the thing he wanted."

But Clint focused on the end of the story and knew that Tom would be anything but satisfied.

TWENTY-EIGHT

"They spelled my name wrong."

Tom and Niestrom sat around a table which looked about ready to collapse under its own weight. They were in the small, two-room shack that Tom had called home for the better part of his life; the smell of eggs and burnt coffee still hanging in the air.

"Is that all you can say?" Niestrom asked. "Did you read this whole thing?"

The paper was spread out on the table in front of Tom, littered with crumbs from the breakfast he'd just finished. "I read the whole thing, John. You'd think that newspaper man could at least—"

Niestrom's fist came slamming down on top of the table. His dented tin mug fell onto the floor and dumped the last couple sips of coffee onto the dirty boards. "Forget about the way they spelled your goddamn name! That story makes it sound like you left that saloon with yer tail stuck between yer legs. You called out the Gunsmith and this is all they could say about it."

Tom looked down at the paper again, focusing on his name in print. Even misspelled, it was still an impressive sight. "John, I don't think—"

"No! You *don't* think. That's your problem, boy. What did I tell you about calling a man out?"

The younger man's face hardened and he took a deep breath. "You're talking to me like a kid again, John. I've been your partner for a while, and I told you I don't like it when you do that."

But Niestrom ignored Tom's words. He was already off on his own line of thought as he got up and started pacing the room. "I gave them the perfect headline. I said you were the devil himself and what do they print instead? They say we were chased out of there. And don't give me any talk about no goddamn ace in the hole! Whatever bitch you thought was on your side probably left you for that Adams anyway."

Now it was Tom's turn to jump up from his chair. His voice trembled with anger when he said, "if you would've let me do things my way, I wouldn't have been chased out of anywhere. You've taught me a lot, but if I'm going to make a name for myself, I need to do things my way."

"Your way?" Niestrom turned to face Tom, locking eyes with the younger man the way two competing rams might lock horns. "You don't have a 'way', boy. I taught you your way. Don't ever forget that."

"I know what this is about. You wanted to take Adams on yourself, didn't you?"

A deadly silence fell upon the cabin. Between the two men, there was a tension in the air that was heavy as thick smoke billowing from a smothered fire. The younger of the two squared his shoulders in reaction to the unspoken challenge which he felt emanating from Niestrom's seething, multicolored eyes.

"You need to back off, John. That's all I'm saying."

Niestrom took in the warning with a slow, subtle nod. "You sure that's all you're saying?"

"For now . . . yes."

The breath that rolled out of Niestrom's throat sounded

something like a low growl. When it tapered off, he re-laxed his posture and nodded again. "Good. You didn't back down," he said approvingly. "If a man's going to be any kind of fighter, he can't ever back down. Not from anyone."

Despite the other man's words, Tom was still reluctant to let himself be placated. "So are you going to let me take Adams my own way?"

Niestrom thought about that for a moment, his eyes moving back to look at the newspaper that was still spread out on the table. "First thing's first. What're you going to do about that?"

"What can I do? The story's already printed. Folks've already read it. I don't see what can be done to stop that."

"Not stop it. *Fix it.*"

"They printed worse things about us when we were thieving down south."

"That didn't matter. Nobody knew who we were and we weren't trying to do anything but get some jobs under our belts. This is different. This is messing with your good name. If you let that go on too long, there ain't no coming back."

"I can't fix this," Tom said while pointing toward the paper. "But I can make sure that tomorrow's edition looks a whole lot better."

Niestrom grinned and slapped Tom on the shoulder. "*Now* you're talking."

Tom soaked up the approval happily. In one well-practiced motion, he drew his Smith and Wesson and snapped the hammer back. His sights were fixed on Clint Adams's name as he said, "All that newspaper man will have to print tomorrow is two words: *Gunsmith* and *dead.*"

TWENTY-NINE

Instead of taking advantage of the lunch served by the hotel, Abby took Clint to a place that she frequented herself. Clint's first question was whether or not she'd seen Tom or Niestrom around there and when she was about to reply, she looked at Clint with a worried expression on her face.

"No," she said. "I don't think they come around much to this part of town. It's too far away from the Yellow Dog or that cathouse next door to it."

"But you've been with Tom before, right?"

"Yes. I told you that."

"And did you take him here afterward?"

They were standing outside the restaurant which only looked slightly bigger than a single-family home. In fact, all that distinguished it from the rest of the nearby houses was the little sign hanging in the window which simply read, HOME COOKING in handwritten letters.

Abby had been just about to walk inside the place when she stopped, turned to face Clint and placed her hands on her hips. "So what are you going to say next, Clint?" she asked angrily. "That I'm some whore who took Tom into her bed because he paid me?"

117

"No. I didn't say that at all."

"But you were about to. So what if I took him into my bed? I'm sure you don't pass the time reading dime novels between visits here yourself. You keep yourself busy and I never think to ask you about who you've been with. Do you think that makes me any less of a lady?"

Clint made an effort to soften his tone. "No. Of course not."

"I was with Tom because the mood struck me and he seemed exciting. It might humble you a bit for you to know that I slept with you for much the same reason."

Taking hold of her and staring directly into her eyes, Clint waited until he was sure he had her attention before talking again. When he was fairly certain she wasn't too worked up to listen, he said, "None of that matters, Abby. I was asking you those questions because once Tom gets a look at that newspaper article, he'll be fit to be tied."

That seemed to take some of the steam from Abby's temper, but not all of it. "Why didn't you just say that to begin with?"

"Because I didn't want to scare you." Giving her a little smirk, Clint added, "Looking back on it, I would have preferred scaring you rather than have you damn near take my head off."

Abby didn't seem to know how to react to that right away. At first, she seemed to be waiting for Clint to say something else worth yelling at. Then, after she realized that he was being sincere, she let her guard down once again. "I'm . . . not used to having men look out for me," she said. "That kind of comes with the territory."

"You choose to socialize with a rough crowd, Abby. Men like Tom may not be worth the trouble."

"But that's what struck me about him. He seemed different than those others. I work at the Yellow Dog some-times . . . serving drinks or entertaining the gamblers mostly . . . but I'm usually there to just hear them talk and see famous men in the flesh.

"You know what? I actually met Doc Holliday once some time ago. And not too long after that, Wyatt Earp passed through. Can you believe that?"

Clint nodded. "Certainly. Where you find one of those two, the other usually isn't too far behind."

"But most folks only get to read about men like that. I got to meet them. I even talked to Doc."

"Plenty of folks come to the Yellow Dog for that same reason," Clint said, his voice suddenly wary. "And plenty of other folks walk into those kind of saloons saying they're famous or bad men. Sometimes it's because they want to feel important and sometimes it's just to get free drinks. Hell, I even found a man pretending to be me one time."

Tilting her head and furrowing her brow in concentration, Abby thought for a couple seconds and started shaking her head as if she'd suddenly grown tired. "I . . . I don't know. The man who said he was Doc might have been some skinny, drunken card player. On second thought, he looked too frail to be Doc Holliday. His cheeks were sunken in and he could barely sit upright sometimes. And after drinking a couple bottles of Dave's whiskey all by himself, he might've said he was anybody."

Clint chuckled slightly and grinned. "Actually, that does sound like Doc. This is a little off his beaten path, but you just described Holliday better than anyone could."

"Really?" Although she looked happy for the moment, the feeling quickly faded. "That doesn't change what happened with Tom. I thought he was different somehow. There was something about him which seemed . . . don't know . . . like he was on the edge."

"He's on the edge all right," Clint said. "In fact, last night he might have stepped right over that edge and onto

the trail he'll be forced to walk for the rest of his life."
More to himself, he added, "However long that might be."

Sensing that Clint's mind was distracted, Abby waited
until it looked as though he was paying attention to her.
"Is that why you didn't kill him at the card game?"

"What?"

"You could have killed him any time you chose. Even
if the sheriff gave a damn about doing his job the right
way, he would've called it self-defense. But you wanted
to talk to him. Everyone else in that place was waiting
for the shots to go off, but I saw you trying to talk to
him. Why would you do that?"

"What kind of a question is that?" Clint asked simply.

"A realistic one, and you know it." Abby waited to see
if Clint would object to that and when he didn't, she went
on. "He wants to kill you, Clint. When I was with him, I
listened to his stories and thought they were exciting and
adventurous, but they didn't seem real somehow. I saw
the look in his eyes when he held that gun of his and
it . . . got my blood flowing. But he really wants to kill
you and it scares the hell out of me."

THIRTY

Clint watched as Abby lowered her head and took a deep breath. He could see the shame seeping into her features and before he could try to make her feel better, she lifted her chin and pulled herself together.

"Even after all those years of living here and being with gunmen of all sorts, I never really thought it was anything but an exciting story everyone was telling. Now, after being with Tom and being with you, it's all rushing to me at just how real everything is.

"It's not just someone pulling a trigger and winning a fight. It's one man taking another man's life . . . forever. And when I saw that fight the other night, all I could think about was that look in Tom's eyes and all I could think about was that he would do his best to kill you. Or . . . you would have to kill him."

When Clint had first met Abby, she'd been just another one of the women hanging on every word a gunman said. He'd met plenty of women like that and knew that they were just attracted to the danger and, in Abby's own words, excitement those men represented. In a perfect world, Clint might have been able to look down on those

121

women, but he knew he was guilty of the same thing, except from the other side of the coin.

He lived his life because he sought out the danger for himself. If he didn't crave excitement, he would probably be a prosperous gunsmith in West Texas with a nice house and a wife. But that life wasn't for him. He loved the life of a wanderer and thrived on putting his well-being on the line for causes he deemed as just.

Women like Abby were too much like him for Clint to think any less of them. Truth be told, Clint saw a certain kind of excitement in them just as they saw it in him. To prove that, all he had to do was look back at all the women he'd been with over the years. Every one of them had a certain spark or some kind of edge to them, whether it be in their personality or their actions.

Because of all of this, Abby knew Clint was being completely truthful when he looked deeply into her eyes and said, "None of this makes you a bad person. Believe me . . . I know."

Hearing that from anyone else might not have done Abby any good. But hearing it from that man at that particular time made all the difference in the world. Suddenly, Abby felt as though a weight had been taken from her shoulders and grateful tears showed at the corners of her eyes.

"Are you sure about that?" she asked.

Clint nodded. "Yeah. I'm sure about that."

The tears were there, but Abby wasn't fully crying. When she swiped at her eyes, she was able to quickly recover from the slip of emotion and regain her composure. "Then if you know what I'm talking about, you should also know why I asked my question before. Why would you try to talk to him when you know Tom is out to kill you?"

"Because I know just as much about those types of men as you do. Actually, I know quite a bit more. And last night, I saw the same kind of thing in Tom that you did. Well," Clint said with a grin, "maybe not *exactly* the same type of thing."

Catching the implication almost before Clint was finished saying it, Abby lightly smacked him on the arm to let him know that she didn't appreciate it.

"I saw that he was on the edge of something," he continued. "But I saw him as being on the verge of becoming either the bad man he so desperately wants to be or a man who'd had his fun and sown his wild oats before settling down for good."

"I think he may be a little further along than that, Clint. Ever since he's been riding with Niestrom, they've been pulling robberies and running from the law from a couple states farther south."

"Maybe, but he hadn't stared another man in the eyes, drawn his gun and killed him yet. I can tell. Anyone who's done that themselves can tell if someone else has been there. It's in their eyes. And once they pull that trigger for that type of reason, it shows in their eyes.

"It shows right at the moment when they're faced with the possibility of doing it again, right at that moment when they might have to kill someone else." When he described it, Clint felt as though he was describing the ghostly faces of so many of those others that he'd seen through the years at the other end of his own weapon.

"There's no fire," he said. "No excitement. Actually, it looks rather cold in there when they're about to kill again. The younger ones show a little bit of fear and maybe a bit of dread. Even the mad dogs look more hungry than excited and the true gunmen's eyes just sort of glaze over because their instinct is taking control and giving them whatever they need to stay alive.

"Then, every so often, you might find a true killer. A real bad man in every respect of the word. They get that look in their eyes that you see in drunks or in those poor souls lying on the floors of opium dens. They look like they *need* to kill. They crave it."

Shaking his head, Clint blinked once or twice and looked at Abby as though he just then started to see her again. "When they're about to kill, they look like that's the moment they've been waiting for their entire lives. The only reason I'm telling you all of this is because that's why I decided to talk to Tom last night rather than just put him down.

"He didn't look like any bad man or mad dog. Not right then, anyway. He looked scared and he looked confused. A little worked up, sure, but no more than anyone else in that place. The only difference is that something tells me if Tom would have killed me, then all those things I saw would've glazed over and he might just become exactly what he says he wants to be."

"And what about now?" Abby asked. "Since he didn't kill you, what happens to him?"

Clint shrugged and said, "I'm going from my gut here. If I could tell you what happens next, I'd make a hell of a living reading palms. What I can tell you is that kid is torn between what he wants and what Third Eye wants for him. Unfortunately, he may still be thinking that he'll find out who he wants to be once he can truly say he's a bad man. Right now, that might be the easiest thing for him to do. And to do that, he'll still have to come after me."

"Which leaves us right where we were before." Abby's voice was a mix of frustration, anger and fear. "Tom wants to kill you and Niestrom is right there lighting a fire under him. If I were you, I'd be more worried about Niestrom than anyone else."

"Don't you worry about Third Eye. He doesn't bother me half as much as Tom."

"But Niestrom is a killer," Abby said in a troubled tone. "He's—"

"He's already picked his trail and is miles along it. That's why I have no question in my mind about what to do the next time I see him. The only thing I regret is not taking him out back at the Yellow Dog. That might have solved a lot of this right then."

"Or it could have given Tom another reason to come after you."

Clint took Abby in his arms and held her tightly for a moment. He then looked into her face and said, "That's what I always liked about you, Abby. You're a good judge of character."

"I don't know about that."

"Well I do." Glancing at the door they'd been standing next to for this entire conversation, Clint reached out and pushed it open. "I also know that I'm still hungry as a bear and could use a break from all this serious talk for a while."

"Now you're talking," Abby said in a way that sounded like her true, carefree self.

Clint let her walk in ahead of him and returned the smile Abby gave him. The moment she turned her back, however, he scanned the street with cold, sharp eyes. There was no excitement in them and no fear. Just the knowledge of what he had to do.

THIRTY-ONE

Dave rarely left the Yellow Dog. He lived in a suite upstairs and felt uneasy whenever he was too far away from his establishment to hear the voices of his customers and the familiar rattle of chair legs scraping across the floor. He didn't even see his job as work. Instead, it was a pleasure to own a saloon and make his living by staying there and pouring drinks.

Dave loved the Yellow Dog. He loved the smell of the alcohol and cigar smoke. He even loved the stale taste of beer on the back of his tongue. He loved dealing with the people who drifted in and out of his doors.

But there were those rare occasions when Dave absolutely hated being the sole proprietor of the Yellow Dog Saloon. When he heard the front door slam open and saw Tom Bolander charge inside, Dave recognized this as one of those moments.

As much as he hated to abandon his post, Dave slowly lowered his head, stepped over the piles of broken glass which had yet to be swept up and prayed he could make it to the back stairs without being seen. He was just about to step out from behind the bar when a voice stopped him quicker than as if a brick wall had been dropped in his path.

"Just where the hell do you think you're goin'?"

The voice was too rough to be Tom's. In fact, the last time Dave had heard it, that same voice had been screaming about the devil outside of his door.

"I'm not going anywhere, John," Dave replied in a casual, albeit slightly shaky, voice. "What can I do for you?"

Niestrom stormed through the back door to the saloon less than a few seconds after Tom had come through the front. Both men were searching the saloon with their eyes, tensed and ready to strike.

"What can you do for me?" Niestrom mocked. "How about a nice glass of whiskey?"

Dave stopped and waited quietly for the next shoe to drop. "Uhhh . . . I can do that for you, sure," he said, sounding more than a little relieved. Glancing toward the bartender standing behind the bar, Dave snapped his fingers and pointed toward Niestrom. "Get this man a drink. On the house, of course."

Waiting until the other man was halfway through the motion of pouring the drink, Niestrom reached out and slapped the glass onto the floor. "No! I want him to do it," the gunfighter said while leveling a finger at Dave.

The Yellow Dog's owner put on a shaky smile and relieved the other bartender of his position. "Go on and see to the rest of the customers. Mister Niestrom probably just wants to talk."

Niestrom's milky-white eye fixed on Dave with a little more clarity than the gray one. The effect was disconcerting and caused the barkeep to look away as he got a fresh glass and started pouring the whiskey.

By this time, Tom had walked over to stand next to Niestrom and leaned his back against the bar. "He ain't here. Not unless he's hiding."

"He ain't hiding," Niestrom said without taking his eyes from the barkeep. "Is he, Dave?"

"Uhh . . . who might you be t—"

"Adams, you little prick!" Niestrom shouted as his hand snapped out to take hold of Dave by the front of his shirt. "Clint Adams. Where is he?"

"H-how should I kn-know? I haven't s-seen him since last night."

"Then tell me where he's staying."

Dave was trying to answer, but his mouth was trembling too hard for him to form the words. When Niestrom pulled him off his feet, Dave tried to grab on to the edge of the bar for support, but his grip fumbled on the polished wood and he only succeeded in knocking over the glass he'd just tried to fill.

Finally, the barkeep was able gather enough breath to squeeze out a couple syllables. ". . . don't know . . . honest," he squeaked.

Moving as slow as a piece of rock sliding through mud, Niestrom turned so he could catch Tom in the corner of his eye. Once the younger man returned his look, the gunfighter nodded almost imperceptibly and looked back at Dave.

In a temperate voice, Niestrom said, "You know something. And you got four seconds to tell me what it is. One . . ."

The barkeep shook his head enthusiastically, his jaw flapping open and shut without a sound coming through.

"Two . . ."

Moving in a little closer, Tom drew his .44 and pointed it at the barkeep's face.

"Three . . ."

The kid thumbed back the hammer. When he heard the dry metallic *click,* the corner of Tom's eye twitched.

". . . Four."

"Wait! I think he said something about—"

Dave was interrupted by a rustle of movement coming from the end of the bar that was closer to the front of the room. The barkeep's eyes waggled like a dog's tail inside their sockets, flicking between the two men in front of him and the source of the motion at the end of the bar.

Tom looked in that direction and immediately spotted the relief bartender lifting a sawed-off shotgun from its place beneath the lowest shelf of whiskey bottles. Although the short man wearing the beer-stained apron seemed only slightly less rattled than Dave, he wasn't having any trouble lifting the weapon and cocking back both hammers.

"Oh, now this is funny," Niestrom said without the first trace of concern drifting onto his face. "Looks like we've got ourselves a man who can sling booze and shoot a gun. He's a real hero, huh Dave?" To Tom, he said, "Put this hero down, kid. Dave here's gonna watch."

Dave shut his eyes tightly, but soon felt the tap of steel beneath his chin. When he opened his eyes again, Niestrom's grinning face was there to meet him.

"I said watch, Dave." The gunfighter took Dave by the hair and twisted until he'd forced the barkeep to look in the proper direction. "So watch. Go on, kid. Let's get on with this show."

THIRTY-TWO

The relief bartender trained his shotgun between Tom and Niestrom. Without taking his eyes from those two, he said, "Somebody fetch the sheriff."

At first, there wasn't a soul in that saloon that was willing to oblige. But one of the locals who'd been sitting at a table near the front door suddenly jumped to his feet and headed for the street. The fleeing man tripped in his haste, fell to his knees and scrambled to get up again.

Tom knew what he was supposed to do. He recognized that man and didn't want to shoot him, but when he saw that he'd made it back to his feet and was about to run, Tom felt desperation pump through his blood, turning it cold in his veins. It was the robber in him more than any kind of killer which caused him to act, since he knew the law would be on its way.

Twisting at the waist and aiming from the hip, Tom squeezed off a shot which blasted through the entire saloon.

The bullet whipped through the air and drove straight for its intended target. Before it touched flesh, however, the man who had been running for the door tripped again

130

over his own fumbling feet; his haste directly responsible for saving his very life.

Hissing like a wasp over the guy's head, the chunk of lead dug a hole in the door frame at the exact spot where the man's head had been less than a second earlier.

Too scared to do anything but scramble on his hands and knees through the door, the man counted his blessings that he was still alive and threw himself into the open air outside the saloon. Once there, he tried to get up again, but could only manage a running stumble which tossed him chin first off the boardwalk and into the dirt below.

The door swung shut just as the man finally managed to get to his feet. When it shut, Tom was still holding the smoking pistol in his hand. Behind him, Niestrom was having a hard time controlling his laughter enough to get a clear word out.

"Sweet Jesus," the gunfighter finally said. "I said I wanted a show, Tom, but *damn!*"

"Shut up, John," the kid replied.

If Niestrom heard Tom's reply, he didn't seem to think much of it. "It doesn't matter, anyway, kid. Let him get the sheriff. Hell, let him get all the deputies too. That's just what we need right about now."

Turning back to face Niestrom, Tom snarled, "What the hell are you going on about now, you crazy bastard?"

Once again, Niestrom didn't seem to take the slightest offense from what Tom was saying. "Adams is the type that likes working with the law dogs. I hear he kisses the ass of anyone who wears a badge, so that just means he'll come running when he sees the law coming back here. And if that don't work, he'll surely come running when he hears that them laws are being pumped full of lead."

Tom shook his head while pressing the palm of his free hand to his temple. "I don't believe this," he said quietly. "This ain't happening."

"Believe it, kid. This is just what you needed to happen.

The law in this town is so soft, I'll bet Dave here could gun half of them down. Ain't that right?" When he asked that question, he jabbed the barrel of his gun a little deeper into the barkeep's chin.

"Y-yessir," Dave replied.

Standing all but forgotten at the other end of the bar, the relief tender still held his shotgun. Only by this time, his hands were trembling and a layer of sweat had started pouring from his scalp and palms. "You men need to get out of here or I'll shoot," the bartender finally said, unconvincingly.

Niestrom glanced in that direction and looked vaguely amused. "Oh, I nearly forgot about you. Tom . . . put that shit heel out of his misery."

All the eyes in the place went to Tom. Besides Niestrom and Dave, there were a few others scattered at some of the tables. After seeing what nearly happened to the one man who'd barely made it out, none of the other customers were about to try their luck. Instead, they helplessly watched the events unfold, waiting for their numbers to come up.

Tom hadn't forgotten about the man with the shotgun. On the contrary, he'd been hoping that one would have tried to make a break for freedom as well. But since he'd stood his ground, the relief bartender was forcing Tom's hand.

Standing there with the warm .44 in his grip, Tom began to wonder what the hell he'd been thinking all these years. Not only had he known a moment like this would be coming, he'd actually been waiting for it. And not only had he been waiting, he'd been waiting *anxiously*.

The more Tom thought about it, the sicker he felt. But he was living through that moment and there was nothing anyone could do about it.

No more than a second or two had gone by, but it was more than enough time for all of those thoughts to fly through Tom's head. Watching him carefully, Niestrom seemed less upset about anything that had happened than he would have been over a bad round of cards.

The gunfighter studied his pupil intently. "You look like your head hurts, kid. Something bothering you?"

Tom could feel the fear radiating from the bartender with the shotgun like waves of heat coming from a pot-bellied stove. He knew that shotgun would be going off soon, either out of fear or even a slip of a finger.

Watching Tom's predicament with no small amount of interest of his own, Niestrom shot Dave a quick wink before slamming the butt of his gun against the top of the bar. He moved without so much as a flinch to announce what he was up to, using the speed in his arm to bring the pistol crashing against the wood.

The resulting sound echoed through the Yellow Dog like a small explosion. Its suddenness made Dave jump half an inch off the floor, but startled the relief bartender even more.

Shoved over the edge of his nerves, the man with the shotgun panicked the moment he heard that sound and reacted out of sheer impulse. His finger tightened around both triggers and set the shotgun off with a roaring blaze.

Tom felt as if everything was happening in slow motion. Already nervous because he'd been forced to shoot with his left hand, he could feel the heat flowing from both of the bartender's barrels and knew that his time on earth was about to come to a crashing halt.

Also reacting on impulse, the kid dropped down and to the side while tensing his finger around the trigger. Fiery pain stung his arm and shoulder as the shotgun blast roared by. Another duller pain jarred his backbone as he landed on the floor.

And all the while, the gun was barking in his grip as if it had taken on a life of its own. When the world looked normal again and the blood stopped rushing through his ears, Tom realized that he hadn't fired a single shot.

Instead, he'd fired all six.

He looked over to the relief bartender who still stood in his spot, holding his spent shotgun and wearing a dumbfounded look on his face. For that instant, Tom actually allowed himself to have some hope.

"Jerry?" Tom asked, finally remembering that other bartender's name. "You all right?"

Jerry blinked, coughed a couple times and spat a wad of blood onto the front of his shirt. Since he'd been wearing black, Jerry had to wipe his palm over himself to see if he was hurt. Before he took his hand away, the blood had seeped through the material, making his clothing look like wet tar. But Jerry didn't get a chance to notice, since his eyes had already clouded over and he dropped to the floor.

"There now," Niestrom said as he stepped away from the bar and looked at Tom. "That wasn't so hard, now was it?"

THIRTY-THREE

Once they'd gotten inside the modest little restaurant, Clint and Abby were able to leave everything they'd been talking about outside so they could enjoy their meal. They'd gotten to order and were just receiving their drinks when they heard some kind of commotion coming from outside.

At first, it sounded like somebody was shouting at a horse to get it to run faster. The person's voice echoed down the street and was accompanied by the clomping of feet. Clint was doing a good job of ignoring it when the voice and the clomping got closer and became something else entirely.

"Do you hear that?" Abby asked.

Clint turned to look toward the front window. "Yeah. It sounds like someone screaming somebody's name."

As he said that, Clint realized that the clomping steps were not coming from a horse, but were actually someone's boots pounding against the boardwalk. The moment he recognized that sound, he got up from his chair and walked over to the window. Just like the outside of the restaurant, the inside looked very much like someone's home. The walls which would have separated a parlor and dining room had been removed, but the lace curtains and family portraits still gave the place a nice, comfortable feel.

Clint walked over to the window and pulled aside the curtains, glancing out at the street, hoping he wouldn't see much of anything. At least that way, he could sit back down and enjoy his meal in good conscience.

But whatever powers were in charge of such things didn't feel like accommodating Clint just then. Come to think of it, Clint was hard-pressed to think of very many times when they had accommodated him.

Standing that close to the glass, Clint could clearly hear the voice as it rolled down the street. Within seconds, the man doing the screaming came thundering by as though his britches were on fire. For a man of his chunky build, the man was moving awfully fast. But this was due to the panic that was reflected in the expression on his face as well as the way he flapped his arms wildly while chugging down the side of the street.

The middle-aged woman who'd taken their order came walking out to stand next to Clint. "What is that fool screaming about?" she asked.

Clint was already on his way to the door. "He's scared out of his mind and screaming for the sheriff. That's never a good combination." Glancing over to Abby, he asked, "Are you going to be all right here by yourself?"

She nodded. "I'll wait here for you."

"You remember what we talked about?"

"Yes." She sighed. "I'll stay here and keep my head down. But if you're going to go charging out there following that commotion, I don't see the point."

"Just humor me."

And with that, Clint walked out the front door and shut it tightly behind him.

The frantic runner had just torn past the restaurant as Clint stepped outside. All it took was a couple of running strides and Clint was able to catch up to him.

"Sheriff! Sheriff! Somebody get the sheriff!" the man screamed breathlessly.

Clint reached out and got hold of the fellow's shoulder. He was trying to shout over what the man was saying, but Clint's voice was completely washed away in the other man's panic. So rather than strain his throat, Clint tightened his grip on the man's shirt and forced him to a stop.

Despite the fact that Clint had a solid hold on him, the man still tried to keep running. He didn't even seem to notice that he was being stopped until his body simply couldn't move forward any longer. After almost tripping over his own feet, the man wheeled around to get a look at who'd taken hold of him, ripping the seam of his shirt in the process.

Reflexively, the man took a swing at Clint while muttering a string of babbled obscenities.

"Whoa, whoa," Clint said as he easily batted the other man's fist aside. "What's the hurry? You need some help?"

Once he saw that he wasn't in any immediate danger, the man stopped struggling and started spilling his guts to Clint. The words spilled out of him like water through a busted dam, but he took a breath and started again.

"There's been a shooting," he said. "Or there will be. They've got guns and they're gonna shoot. One of them took a shot at me. I need to find the sheriff."

"Where is all this happening?"

"At the Yellow Dog. That kid, Tommy and Third Eye Niestrom. They're about to shoot the place up. They got Dave and I think I heard shots after I left."

"They shot at you?"

"Hell yes, they did. When I tried to get out of there, one of them took a shot at me. I think it was Tommy, but I can't hardly believe it. He doesn't seem like the killer type. I think they might want to rob the place."

Clint was looking in the direction the man had been running and quickly spotted the sheriff's office. He was just about to tell the guy to keep running that way and do what he was set to do when the man broke in again.

"They were after someone," he sputtered. After thinking for a second, his face lit up. "Adams. Niestrom said he wanted to know where Clint Adams was, but Dave wouldn't tell him."

"He didn't tell him because he didn't know."

"What makes you say that?"

"Because I didn't tell him."

That was all the man had to hear before he put two and two together. Suddenly, the panic returned to his face and he looked at Clint with wide, staring eyes. "You're Adams! Oh, hell, they're after you. And I'm . . ."

"Go on," Clint said, rather than make the other man say what was on his mind. "Go get the sheriff and tell him what's going on."

"But he probably won't want any part of Niestrom."

Clint let go of the man and started jogging down the street for the Yellow Dog. "Then tell him to stay out of the way."

THIRTY-FOUR

The inside of the Yellow Dog Saloon had been quiet as a tomb since the shooting had stopped. With Jerry still lying in a bloody heap behind the bar, the rest of the customers were keeping their mouths shut and trying their best not to move a muscle.

Tom didn't look much different. After stepping up to the bar, he'd set his foot on the rail and leaned on his elbows as if he was quietly contemplating his whiskey. But his eyes were trained at the dead body behind the bar. The kid's mind spun as he took in the sight of all that blood soaking into the floorboards.

"You see," Niestrom said. "All you ever have to do is put one man down and everyone else falls into line."

Tom didn't say a word. He was still reeling from the aftermath of what he'd done.

Niestrom looked over at him and asked, "What's the matter, kid? I thought this is just where you wanted to be."

"This ain't nowhere near where I wanted to be."

Laughing once, Niestrom moved away from the bar and walked over to where Tom was standing. Once he'd taken a few steps in that direction, Dave let out a haggard breath and nearly collapsed against the shelves behind him.

"It can't all be talking in bars and impressing ladies," Niestrom said plainly. "A man can only lie so much before he reaches his end. Besides that, a true bad man don't have to lie." The gunfighter lowered his voice and got close enough so that only Tom could hear him speak. "That's what this is all about. When this is over, these here folks are gonna talk. And when they do, they'll make you out to be some kind of goddamn demon. Talk like that is what makes a man. You get enough of that going for you and folks'll be shitting their britches when we pull another job. They'll throw their money at you just so you'll leave them alone."

"How come they never did that to you on any of our jobs?" Tom asked.

"Because we hid our faces. You can't learn nothing if I walk in and do all the work. I think I carried you too far as it is," he added in a grunting tone. "You're too damn soft."

Tom shook his head and peeled his eyes away from the body staring up at the ceiling. "You're crazy, John."

"Maybe. But just wait till this is over. You'll see I'm right."

Both men stared at each other for a few moments. Niestrom was letting his words soak into the younger man's skull, knowing that what he said would make sense eventually. Tom studied the gunfighter for some trace of rational thought. When he didn't see any right away, he wondered what the hell had possessed him to hook up with Niestrom in the first place.

"Look here," Niestrom said from out of nowhere. He turned toward the tables and walked for the closest one that was occupied. Grabbing the first customer he could find, he hauled a gray-haired man to his feet and glared into his face. "Who am I?"

The customer looked confused for a second, but managed to find his voice. "John Niestrom."

"What do they call me?"

"Th-Third Eye."

Leaning in a little closer, Niestrom started to raise his pistol and snarled, "And why do they call me that?"

Clenching his eyes shut, the customer began trembling. His breathing came in quick, shallow gulps and sweat broke out on his forehead. "J-J-Jesus. No . . . don't . . . please . . ."

Niestrom smiled and dropped the man back into his seat. "You see there?" he said to Tom. "He knows who I am and what I do. More than that, he knows I'm a killer. And if some shit kicker like this knows, that means there's plenty of men out there that matter who know as well. That's what this is about, kid. And if I have to tell you that one more time, I swear to God, I'll—"

"He's here!"

Niestrom and Tom both snapped their heads around to get a look at who had just said that. They found one of the other card players peering through the window and pointing excitedly at the glass.

"Who's here?" Tom asked.

Ignoring the glare from Niestrom, the card player replied, "Clint Adams. I saw him at the game last night and now he's coming up the street."

Niestrom went to the window and took a look for himself. Nodding slowly, he gazed at the street and allowed his familiar smile to creep back onto his face. "Yeah. That's him all right."

Dave started to run out from behind the bar, but stopped before he got anywhere near Tom. The barkeep skidded to a halt and moved toward the center of the room so he could see out the window as well. "Is that really him, Darryl?"

"It sure is," the card player answered.

"Is the sheriff here too?"

It was Niestrom who decided to answer that particular question. "There ain't no law out there. And there won't be, since the law in this town is too yellow to do anything but roust drunks and check the locks on doors. It's our time to shine, Tom."

The kid took a deep breath and let it out. Although it didn't help to settle his stomach, he was able to walk over to the window without faltering in his step. Despite the fact that he was no longer looking at the relief bartender's body, he could still see that bloody corpse as clearly as if the image had been burned into his retinas.

Tom was wondering how he could possibly get himself out of this situation, but was unable to come up with a solution in the seconds it took for him to get to the window. But something happened to the kid when he stepped up to the glass and looked outside. He realized at that moment that he couldn't possibly get out of the situation.

It was too late for that.

All he could do was deal with the direction his life had taken and pay for all those times he'd said he wanted to be a true bad man.

"You ready, kid?" Niestrom asked without even trying to mask the excitement in his voice.

"Yeah," Tom said with his newfound clarity. "I'm ready."

THIRTY-FIVE

Clint flew down the street without even seeing the faces or buildings he passed along the way. He didn't have to see the locals scattered along the boardwalk to know what they were thinking or how they would be looking at him. Since he was tracking back over the other man's frantic footsteps, Clint knew that the people here would already be talking about what was going on.

They might even know more about it than he did.

But Clint didn't have to stop and ask any of them, no matter how helpful it could have been. What he needed to do was get to the Yellow Dog before anyone got hurt.

He winced when he realized the error in that thought.

Before anyone *else* got hurt.

Knowing that some innocent bystander had been hurt by that fool Niestrom only made Clint move faster. He thought that one would be content stewing for a while after what had happened the night before. Men like him usually took their defeats hard. In fact, Clint thought that Niestrom would have kept his head low for a while and that Tom would be the one to worry about.

Clint figured that the kid would still want to make a name for himself, but wouldn't do so at the cost of someone's life. After summing Tom up with his own eyes, Clint figured that the kid would just need some time to cool his heels.

And because of that, Clint had done his best to keep Abby safe while he got something to eat.

Being wrong never sat too well in Clint's gut. Being this wrong felt like a kick from an angry mule.

By the time the Yellow Dog was in sight, Clint felt his own rage churning to the surface like bile in the back of his throat. He knew better than to let something like that get over on him, but choking it down was no easy task. He forced himself to slow his steps and take a moment to breathe.

The fire died down slightly behind his eyes and he stepped in front of the saloon with an easy, confident stride.

"Lord above," Clint thought. "Dave will be talking about this one for the rest of his natural life."

Clint didn't bother calling out Niestrom and Tom right away, figuring that those two would be more than happy to come out on their own. He wasn't disappointed.

The door to the Yellow Dog flew open and smacked against the frame. Surprisingly enough, Niestrom wasn't the first man to walk outside. Tom did the honors, stepped from the saloon and moved aside so that Third Eye could follow.

"Glad you showed, Adams," Tom said. "You saved me the trouble of coming after you."

Clint locked eyes on the kid and found that his initial fears had come true. The Tom Bolander that had dragged his feet like a reluctant child going to church was now walking tall and making no excuses. What told Clint the most, however, was the fact that Tom didn't turn away from Clint's gaze.

He met it head-on. Tom even held it for a few seconds so he could add some heat of his own.

"Is this how you hunt down a man?" Clint asked. "By sitting around some saloon and stirring up enough shit to draw him out? I'm surprised the sheriff wasn't the only one to respond to those kind of brilliant tactics."

Tom shrugged. "If the law had shown up, I would've gunned him down and had another drink."

"That easy, huh?" Moving as if to look beyond the two gunmen, Clint nodded toward the Yellow Dog. "I heard you might've shot a man in there, Tom. Is that true?"

That definitely hit a nerve in the younger man. It only showed as a brief flicked across his face, but shone through to Clint's eyes as another crack in the wall the kid had built around himself.

"Just a barkeep who was too dumb to know when to stay still," Tom said.

"Dave?"

"It don't matter." Tom stepped forward and walked down from the boardwalk until both his boots landed on the street. "All that matters is that you've got to deal with me now."

Clint then looked at Niestrom. "Is that what ol' Third Eye told you?"

Tom's jaw tensed, but no words came in answer.

"Because if you're still listening to him, then you've obviously chosen the wrong teacher." Although he was only watching Niestrom from the corner of his eye, Clint could almost see the anger seething from the older gunfighter. "He may do a lot of talking, but that's because he's never been much good at anything else."

Niestrom's eye twitched as if it was attached to a string. Soon, his lips were pulling taut over uneven teeth.

"Forget about John," Tom said. His voice sounded stronger now. Compared to the way he'd carried himself at the poker game, this might as well have been an entirely different person. "You're talking to me now."

Clint smirked in a way that he knew would raise the

hackles on the back of Niestrom's neck. "Forgetting about Niestrom won't be too hard. Especially since nobody's ever even heard of him in the first place."

Tom must have been able to feel the heat coming from Niestrom as well. Because although it was plain enough to see that he had more to say, he held his tongue and took a quick look over his shoulder. If he'd been hoping to soothe Niestrom's nerves before they boiled over, he was about two seconds too late.

"What the fuck do you know Adams?" Niestrom exploded as he stepped forward and pushed Tom aside. "I made my own way by blowing the brains out of pigs like you. One right through the skull . . . that's all it takes. Even for a Gunsmith . . . that's all it fuckin' takes."

Tom tried to stop him, but Niestrom shook off the kid's hand and limped another step forward. "You ain't nothin'. Big, bad Gunsmith and all you can do is talk. Well you talked too much, bad man, and now it's gonna cost ya."

Clint took a slow step back, figuring that Niestrom wouldn't hesitate to close the gap. He wasn't disappointed.

THIRTY-SIX

Clint might not have been much of an actor, but he could do well enough to fool a certain kind of audience. Namely, it had to be the kind of audience that was aching to see what they wanted to see, no matter what was going on upon the stage.

Stepping back, Clint only had to let his eyes drift slightly off target to get Niestrom to believe that he was backing down. Anyone in their right mind might have thought twice about such a thing, but Niestrom had been pushed out of his right mind by the short exchange with Clint.

More than anything, Niestrom wanted to make Clint Adams afraid.

And all Clint had to do was give him a taste of that to bring the gunfighter out exactly where he wanted him.

Grinning widely, Niestrom narrowed his mismatched eyes and rolled his head upon his shoulders. A series of cracks came from his bones and he lowered his hand to the gun at his side. "Hate to do this to you, kid," he said without looking over his shoulder. "But I'm going to have to take this one myself."

Clint glanced over Niestrom's shoulder and spotted no

fewer than a dozen faces peering out from the Yellow Dog's window. Since he could sense the gunshots coming, Clint backed away even farther and stepped into the street.

Only too willing to follow, Niestrom hobbled across the packed dirt in a way that showed he wasn't a stranger to having to move in less than prime condition. In an odd sort of way, the gunfighter appeared to be more at ease with his injury and the odd angle of his back made the distasteful look that was permanently embedded on his face look a little more at home.

By the time Clint had gotten himself situated in the middle of the street, he saw that he'd attracted a good-sized audience of locals. The onlookers were of all shapes and sizes, attracted by word of mouth, which had no doubt been spread by the same frantic voice that had brought Clint to this very spot.

Niestrom flicked his hand out in dramatic fashion, a move obviously meant more for the crowd than anything else. With a snap of his wrist, he flipped open his coat to fully reveal the holster strapped around his waist. The ornate, gold-plated handle of a .38 revolver poked out from soft, tooled leather.

"You ain't got much to say now, do ya, Adams?" Niestrom asked with a leering grin.

Clint merely shook his head.

Some of the energy in Niestrom's grin was wiped away at the sight, but that didn't stop him from continuing with his own little presentation. "I'm gonna be famous," the gunfighter stated. "After I kill you, there won't be no one in this country that won't know who I am."

"I couldn't give a rat's ass whether or not people know you, Third Eye. If you decide to walk away from this, all you have to do is throw down that gun and do it. If you'd rather die, then pull that weapon and go to work."

Niestrom shifted his weight from one foot to another.

The motion sent a ripple of pain through his lower body
from the fresh wound in his leg. From there, the pain
surfaced as an unsteady snarl tugging at the corner of his
upper lip.

Although Clint wondered about what Tom might be
doing, he knew better than to keep track of the kid with
more than the periphery of his vision. He watched for any
suspicious motion out of the corner of his eye. Any more
than that, and Clint might just give John Niestrom the
fame he so badly desired.

"What'll it be, Third Eye?" Clint asked as the seconds
continued to drag on.

For some reason, hearing his nickname come from
Clint's mouth never failed to annoy Niestrom. That was
the only reason Clint did it. Every time he said those two
words, Clint saw a spark behind Niestrom's eyes. It had
started out as a way to rattle the other man during the
poker game. Now, it was a way to get Niestrom to make
his move. Every second that wasted brought Tom Bolander farther down the road to damnation.

Finally, Niestrom simply couldn't take it anymore. In
a fit of rage, his emotions finally overpowered what little
common sense was inside his brain.

"You can't call me that," the gunfighter said as his hand
clapped around the handle of his gun.

Niestrom's body twisted slightly while his arm brought
the .38 up and out of its resting place. His thumb cocked
the hammer back just as the barrel drew a line to its target.
And though the draw was faster than Clint might have
expected . . . it wasn't fast enough.

Standing like he'd been carved from stone, Clint never
took his eyes away from Niestrom. He'd been waiting
right up to the last minute for the other man to do the
right thing. But instead, Niestrom had gone for his gun.

Clint's arm was the only part of him that moved. His
breathing stopped for half a second. His eyes never left

Niestrom's face. Even the wind seemed to stand still around him as his modified Colt cleared leather and sent a single shot through the air.

That round closed the gap between Clint and Niestrom in less time than it took to blink. The chunk of hot lead dug its path through Niestrom's flesh. The sound of the shot still rumbled like distant thunder up and down the street. Niestrom wobbled on his feet, staring blindly at Clint with his mismatched eyes: one gray, one milky-white, and one dark red in the center of his forehead.

Clint watched as the gunfighter dropped to his knees and let the .38 slide from his fingers. "At least you should be happy about one thing, Third Eye. None of these folks should forget that name of yours."

THIRTY-SEVEN

When Clint knew it was safe for him to take his eyes off of Niestrom, he looked to the spot where Tom Bolander had last been standing. Not only was the kid not in that spot, but he wasn't even anywhere that Clint could see.

Every one of Clint's muscles tensed as he prepared himself to be attacked from any angle. The Colt was in his hand, ready to fire. All he needed was a target. But the kid still didn't show. That was when Clint's nerves really started to fray.

Clint broke into a quick stride and headed for the Yellow Dog's front door. Although he wanted to run into the saloon, he didn't want to run headlong into an ambush. His eyes soaked up every detail around him as he climbed onto the boardwalk and pushed open the saloon's door. All he could see was a whole lot of wide-eyed locals lining the street and peering out through nearby windows. None of those folks said a word to Clint as he walked into the Yellow Dog and the few that were in his way quickly jumped to one side to let him pass.

The door pushed open easily enough, swinging on oiled hinges to reveal the inside of the Yellow Dog. Clint stood his ground for a moment before stepping inside, still taking his time in the name of caution. Since his own heart was pounding inside his chest, he was certain the kid's must be about to jump out of his mouth.

Since there was hardly any sign of motion inside the saloon, not to mention any trace of a frantic gunman, Clint stepped inside. The first thing that caught his attention was the smell of stale gunpowder hanging in the air, mixed with the unmistakable stench of spilled blood.

Suddenly, there was a burst of motion coming from the bar. Clint twisted on the balls of his feet, preparing himself to fire if necessary.

"Don't shoot," Dave said while raising his hands. "It's only me."

Clint allowed himself to relax a bit and lowered his pistol. "Where's Tom?" The moment that question left his mouth, Clint saw the section of shelves behind the bar that had been knocked apart. All it took was a quick glance behind the slab of polished wood for him to spot the crumpled figure of the relief bartender who was still grasping his shotgun with both hands.

Dave was careful not to look at the body as he walked over to stand beside Clint. He even went so far as to clench his right eye shut so he wouldn't have to catch so much as a peek of the carnage. "Tom left with Niestrom before you got here. Or maybe that was right about the same time you got here."

"What about after that?" Clint asked. "I saw him outside, but Tom's not there anymore. Where did he go?"

One of the locals sitting at a card table within sight of the front window crawled out from where he'd been hiding. He also held his hands up in the air and approached cautiously.

At that moment, Clint couldn't help but feel as though he was robbing the Yellow Dog rather than trying to clear out its bad element.

"I saw the kid take off," the local man said. "Watched

the whole thing from the window ... well ... what I could see from where I was hidin'."

Clint looked over to that man and asked, "Where did he go?"

"He started to come back in here right before that first shot was fired. I saw him turn and look at the street ... that was right about when Third Eye was dropping to the ground. Then the kid ducked off to the right and I lost sight of him."

As soon as he heard that, Clint ran for the door again and poked his head outside. Sure enough, there was an alley to the right of the door that was no more than eight or ten feet away. With all that was going on in his fight with Niestrom, Clint could very well have missed seeing Tom take off in that direction.

Before Clint was able to leave the saloon, he heard that same local speak up again.

"That was a hell of a thing you did, mister. My thanks to you. We all owe you our thanks."

Clint nodded to acknowledge the sentiment. Before his chin could lift up after that first nod, the saloon was filled with a sound he most certainly had never been expecting. It started off as a smattering here and there, but soon the applause filled the room, accentuated by the occasional whistle.

Letting out a heavy sigh, Clint turned away from his adoring public and headed for the alley. On the way, he couldn't help but think that no matter how disturbed or deluded John Niestrom had been, he had his head straight about one thing.

If anyone was to make a name for themselves through word of mouth, the Yellow Dog Saloon was the place to do it.

Before Clint had even jumped off the boardwalk, the people inside were getting up and dusting themselves off while swapping stories about what part of the gunfight they'd witnessed.

THIRTY-EIGHT

The space that Clint stepped into was less of an alleyway and more of a narrow passage that just happened to be between two buildings. There wasn't even enough room for him to walk in normally, which forced him to turn sideways and wedge himself in that way.

Even so, he still couldn't move at full speed since either his back or front was scraping along the side of a building as he moved toward the other side of the passage. It was slow going, but Clint took some measure of comfort from the fact that Tom would have had just as much trouble. The kid probably had a harder time since he was trying to make the short trip a lot faster than Clint.

Knocking his head on the wall behind him, Clint took a look upward to check if there was any chance that there might be danger from above. The roofs on either side sloped to within an inch of each other, making it next to impossible for anyone to get much of a shot if they'd climbed up there hoping to pick him off.

But Clint really didn't think that Tom was about to do such a thing. On the other hand, he wasn't exactly sure what Tom was about to do, either. That wasn't from any lack of possibilities, though. If the kid wanted to run or make a stand, either choice wouldn't seem too far from the realm of possibility.

And depending on which of those choices he took, the kid might do any number of things ranging from different ways out of town to any number of plans of attack to finish the job Niestrom had started. Just thinking about it was beginning to make Clint's head swim. So rather than bother himself with going back and forth on maybes, he decided to focus in on what he knew for sure.

At that moment in time, Clint knew for sure that Tom had taken off in this direction and that he needed to catch up with the kid as soon as possible. He also knew that if he'd had much more of the lunch he'd ordered with Abby, he might very well have been stuck in between those buildings until one of them burned down.

Although neither of the structures were poorly built, neither of them had been made perfectly level. And when they were this close together, every quarter of an inch made a world of difference. Especially to a man trying to shimmy between them.

Clint found himself wedged somewhere just past three-quarters of the way through. His gun belt caught on the wall behind him. When he shifted to free it, the damn thing got caught on the wall in front. Try as he might, Clint was unable to pull himself free. Using his hands to feel the walls on either side, he quickly figured out that the buildings simply came together at a slight angle toward the back.

The good news was that, as far as he could tell, the angle didn't get much worse than it did right where he was standing. Also, he only had another five or six feet to go before he made it to the other side.

The bad news was that Clint still couldn't take more than another step or two before he had to either work his way back out the way he'd come or find some way to make himself thinner.

He tried sucking in his gut, but that was only good for another foot and a half. Muscling through the cramped space only got him a couple bruises to show for his efforts, which left him with only two real choices. And since his natural inclination was to move forward rather than back, Clint took a step or two back just to give himself some space so he could work the buckle of his gun belt.

The holster fell off in a few practiced motions. Clint didn't like the feel of removing the Colt when he might be heading straight for a desperate kid with a gun of his own, but he wasn't about to leave the pistol behind. Instead, he kept the holster dangling from his left hand while flattening himself against one wall and shuffling toward the closest end of the passage. He gripped the Colt in his right hand, pointing it in the direction he was moving.

Moving in that fashion, Clint was able to make quicker progress through the cramped alley. Finally, after smacking damn near every part of himself against one of those two walls, he emerged on the other side. As soon as he could, he strapped the holster back around his waist and searched his surroundings for any trace of the kid.

"I could've taken a shot at you when you came out of there," Tom said from somewhere in the Yellow Dog's back lot.

Clint looked around, but couldn't see Tom anywhere. He did have a good idea of where he was hiding by where the voice was coming from, however. "And I could've saved myself some time by going around a different way," he replied.

Although Clint waited for Tom to speak again, the younger man's voice didn't seem to be forthcoming. To get the kid to open his mouth again, Clint said, "Niestrom's dead, you know."

"Yeah . . . I know."

"Then why are you still here?"

There was no reply.

"Want to know what I think?" Clint asked, focusing in on a stack of crates to his right. That was where Tom's voice had come from, so that was where Clint faced. He didn't move in that direction, however. Not yet.

Clint kept his voice loud enough to be heard, but low enough for him to hear any move the kid might be making. "I think you got in over your head. You and Niestrom did some robberies, but if anyone got hurt, it was accidental. You had your fun and you wanted to make your entire life as exciting as those days you spent running from the law and doing whatever the hell you pleased." Clint waited for a few moments so he could listen to every little sound around him. "Am I right?"

"Yeah," Tom said as he popped up from behind those crates. "I guess you're right."

The kid was clutching his .44 as though it had been melted into his hand. He stared down the gun's barrel and placed his thumb on the hammer.

THIRTY-NINE

Nothing about the move had caught Clint off guard. In fact, his only reaction to it was to adjust his eyes so that he was staring directly at Tom's face. His modified Colt was ready, but it wasn't pointed at any particular target. Although that would have added a fraction of a second onto his time, Clint didn't concern himself with it.

"You can turn this around, Tom. It's not too late."

"That's not the way I see it, Mister Adams. I'm a killer now. There ain't much for me to do but run with it or rot in a cell. That's what John was trying to tell me the whole time." The shadow of regret passed over Tom's face like clouds blocking the daylight. "I never listened to him when I should have. But now I can do what I need to do. At least this way I'll make a name for myself."

Shaking his head, Clint said, "Aren't you forgetting something?" His hand stayed right where it was, keeping the Colt close to his side. "Killing me may get you some sort of fame, but I'm not about to just stand here and let you do it."

Strictly speaking, Tom had the drop on Clint simply because his gun was already drawn and aiming at its target. All that was left for him to do was snap the hammer back and pull the trigger, a move that would take even a modest gunman less than a second to accomplish.

But Tom didn't feel like he had the upper hand in this situation. On the contrary, he was starting to feel like he'd been stuck with the short end of the stick no matter how many advantages he had. Niestrom's words still shot through his mind, urging him to take his chance while he had it.

Things would never get any better than this.

Fire that damn gun, boy!

Tom felt like the gunfighter was still alive and screaming at him in the same voice he'd used when he was alive. And though Third Eye Niestrom was nothing more than an ornery memory, the effect he had on Tom was still the same.

Another voice broke in on the conflict raging on inside Tom's head. This one was quieter, calmer, but somehow less powerful, despite the fact that it wasn't coming from within the kid's mind.

"I don't like staring down gun barrels, Tom," Clint said in a tone that was colder than the bottom of a frozen river. "You can either put it down or be treated like the rest of the men that drew down on me."

Clint wasn't the type to brandish his reputation so openly, but his words had had the exact effect he'd been hoping for. They seemed to rattle Tom right down to the core, causing the gun in his hand to waver ever so slightly.

Suddenly, the kid made his move.

At the first sign of motion, Clint reflexively brought the Colt up to bear on what little of a target he could see. But even that disappeared as Tom took a step back and ducked back down under his cover.

Every one of Clint's senses was on alert, waiting to see if Tom was about to jump out from behind the crates, shoot through them, or even try to push them down toward him. But none of those things happened as Clint started circling around the crates to the right.

His reflexes drawn taut as a bow string, Clint moved slowly in that direction. He could see that faint wavering of a shadow, which told him that Tom was indeed moving behind those boxes. In the next moment, he heard the rattle of something bumping against the wooden crates. That sound was followed by feet scrambling on loose dirt and hasty footsteps taking off in the opposite direction.

Just to be sure, Clint placed his hand on the stack of crates and shoved them over, jumping around to look behind them as they toppled down. As he'd suspected, Tom was already gone. The only path open to him was the rear entrance of the building next to the Yellow Dog.

Clint bolted toward that building, his hand reaching out to catch the door which still rattled on its hinges after Tom had thrown it open. He kept his head low and stepped away from the opening as quickly as he could, still uncertain as to whether or not the kid might take a shot at him. But the sound of running footsteps were echoing through the building and Clint's instincts told him that those were still the kid's feet doing all that moving.

The room Clint had charged into appeared to be some sort of storage area. There were more boxes stacked along one wall, only these appeared to be full. The rest of the room was littered with dusty furniture and stacks of brooms and such. Just like the door leading out the back, the door leading farther into the building had obviously been pushed open. In fact, that one was only swinging on one set of hinges since the other set had been separated from the wall.

Holding the Colt in front of him, Clint moved through the next door and found himself in a short hallway. He could hear the sounds of women screaming and glasses shattering on the floor. It was at this moment that Clint realized he was inside the cathouse which sat next to the Yellow Dog.

Clint moved swiftly but carefully, tracking the obvious signs of where the kid had gone while keeping himself on the lookout for any ambush that might have been set up in his honor. Everytime he saw what looked like a face peeking out from behind a door or around a corner, Clint aimed in that direction.

All he uncovered was a few petrified whores and just as many of their wide-eyed customers. He kept moving through the cathouse, making a straight line, which ended at the place's front door. Once there, Clint saw that that door had been forced open as well. He emerged onto the front porch and found several scantily dressed ladies hiding behind a table and a set of rocking chairs, glancing nervously between Clint and a spot across the street.

"He went that way," one of the ladies offered.

Clint looked and caught a fleeting glimpse of Tom's back as it disappeared in yet another alley across the street. The kid was even faster than he'd thought, and Clint leapt off the boardwalk even though he knew he didn't stand much of a chance in catching him if he didn't do it in the next couple of seconds.

Pouring every last bit of strength into his legs, Clint crossed the street and charged into the alley, making sure he didn't charge into another tight fit like the one he'd so recently experienced. But the kid was nowhere to be seen. The only trace Clint could find was the dust that had been kicked up by Tom's boots as he'd all but flown down to the opposite end of the alley.

Clint knew better than to try and go after him. Not only was Tom younger and lighter on his feet, but he was probably more familiar with this town and had already planned an escape route if the need for one ever arose. Clint at least gave John Niestrom enough credit as a teacher to instill that bit of sense into his pupil's head.

"Damnit," Clint swore as he slammed his fist against the side of the closest building.

By this time, all the adrenaline that had been keeping Clint moving was starting to back up inside his veins. It felt as though his blood was still pumping at twice the speed even though his body had come to a stop. What resulted was a headache, which hit him like a two-by-four in the back of the skull.

Clint could feel his heart slamming inside his chest and took a moment to take in a few deep breaths and force his system to slow down a bit. Once he didn't feel as though he was about to climb out of his own skin, he dropped the Colt back into its holster and started walking back toward the Yellow Dog.

Even if Tom didn't show up there again soon, Clint had another fine reason for returning to that place.

"I need a drink," he muttered.

FORTY

Stepping back into the Yellow Dog, Clint looked around the place and couldn't believe what he saw. His blood had slowed to its normal speed and his heart was no longer racing in his chest, so he knew he couldn't be delirious. His eyes and ears were working fine, so he couldn't blame anything on them either.

With this in mind, Clint walked inside and shut the door, which was still moving unsteadily upon its hinges. He walked up to the bar, set his foot upon the rail and took another look around.

"I'll be damned," he said to himself.

If he didn't know any better, Clint might have thought that this was just another typical day for Dave and his saloon. Sure, he was short one relief bartender, but other than that the place seemed to be working fine. In fact, there were even more people drinking now than when he'd left a couple minutes ago.

Sure, some of the drunks were drinking a little faster and Dave was several shades paler than normal, but there wasn't a whole lot of difference besides that. Just to make sure that he hadn't waken up from a bad dream, Clint glanced behind the bar at the spot where Jerry's body had been.

The corpse was gone, but the dark-red stain was still soaked into the floorboards.

"What can I get for ya?" another of Dave's relief bartenders asked. When Clint looked up, the man behind the bar flinched slightly and put on an expression bordering on awe. "Oh, it's you Mister Adams."

Dave had already caught sight of Clint and was on his way over. "Anything that man wants is on the house."

"Just a beer," Clint said to the bartender closest to him. To Dave, he asked, "What the hell's going on here?"

Although Dave tried to look around as though he wasn't sure what Clint was talking about, he didn't pull off the act too well at all. "Not a lot. At least, not anymore."

"Exactly. So once you sweep up the bodies and mop up some of the blood around here, everything just goes right back to normal?"

"What should I do, Mister Adams? Close up and not open my doors until Jerry's cold in the ground?"

"A little respect would be nice. Hell, even a hanged man gets a moment of silence after the trapdoor opens. You all act like nothing happened here today except for a floor show."

Dave's eyes darted reflexively to the dark stain on the floor near his feet. Seeing that, his skin turned a little paler as well as a little sweatier. "This wasn't no floor show," he said in a hushed voice. Dave waited for the other bartender to set Clint's drink down and walk away before he went on. "I haven't been able to catch my breath since it happened. Look . . . I'm still shaking." To illustrate his point, Dave held out one hand palm-down in front of Clint. He was trembling so hard that it almost looked as though some unseen force was moving his arm about in irregular patterns.

"Don't you care that one of your own men is dead?"

Dave let out a troubled sigh. "Sure I do, but . . . you've been in plenty of saloons, Clint. You know that places don't shut their doors after a fight. Folks that know about this place expect to see things like that, even if it don't really happen all that often. And when it does, they'll move on and tell the story to their friends."

Clint didn't think the other man was putting on an act, but he also wasn't too impressed by what he'd seen. More than that, he realized that his words were falling on deaf ears. Dave wasn't any different than any saloon owner. More drinks sold meant that life was good, plain and simple.

"Nobody'll forget what happened here," Dave said. "We owe you more than we can repay. It's all anyone can talk about as a matter of fact. Even the sheriff was talking about the way you and Niest—"

"The sheriff?" Clint interrupted. Hearing that word had made the blood burn in Clint's veins and his temper flare like a kerosene-soaked blaze inside his chest.

Judging by the look on Dave's face, the barkeep was totally aware of the change inside Clint and started instinctually backing up a few steps. "There won't be no charges filed," Dave said in an attempt to pacify the man in front of him.

"You're damn right there won't be any charges filed. I should get a piece of the man's salary since I did the job that was rightfully his in the first place."

Dave held his hands out in front of him and tried to make the best of the situation. Before he could even get started, however, the barkeep was cut off by Clint's finely edged voice.

"Where is he?" Clint asked.

"Right over there, at the table in the back."

FORTY-ONE

Glancing over in that direction, Clint quickly picked out the lawman's face from the middle of a good-sized crowd. By the looks of it, the sheriff was swapping stories with the rest of the ghouls, having a good laugh about the drama they'd seen.

Clint picked up his beer, downed a healthy swig and made his way over to where the town's law was sitting. Along the way, he received plenty of pats on the back and encouraging words from many of the same people who'd been shaking in their boots not too long ago. The entire scene was almost unreal in Clint's eyes and the only way he kept his temper in check was by completely ignoring the words and pats that came his way.

When he got to the lawman's table, Clint found that everyone there was already staring up at him as if they were gazing upon the president himself.

"Can I have a word with you, sheriff?" Clint asked.

"Of course, Mister Adams. Take a seat."

Glancing at all the others seated there, Clint said, "Alone."

Grudgingly, the others got up and moved away from the table. They didn't try to hide the fact that the new

166

spots they'd found were easily within earshot of the ones they'd left.

"Congratulations for a job well done, Mister Adams," the sheriff said while extending his hand. "May I call you Clint?"

Clint didn't shake the lawman's hand, nor did he return the beaming smile. "No, sir. Mister Adams is just fine."

"Suit yourself. What can I do for you?"

Leaning in so that his elbows were resting on the table, Clint said, "I'll make this short. What are you going to do about the man who was killed?"

The sheriff looked as though he didn't know what Clint could possibly be upset about. "You shot down Mister Niestrom yourself. There's a reward which you're entitled to if that's—"

"And what about Tom Bolander?"

"I'll put together a posse and get after him. No need for you to concern yourself."

"And meanwhile, you sit in here and have your drinks?"

The sheriff lifted his glass and tipped it as though Clint had offered a toast. "Like I said, no need to concern yourself."

Clint nodded slowly and looked around to the other men who had been at the table with the sheriff. All of those eyes were still trained on him, watching his every move. "I'll worry about what to concern myself with, sheriff. But I'll tell you one thing that this whole town should be concerned with, and that's a sheriff that lets shootings go on right under their noses and doesn't do anything about it because they might scare away sight-seers.

"Then again, that might not be the case with you, either. You couldn't be corrupt because if that was the case, I'm sure Niestrom would have come after me a lot sooner. Plus, I don't see Dave as the type to buy off the law.

"You know where that leaves me, sheriff?" Clint asked. "It leaves me thinking that what I heard about you the first time was the absolute truth. Your only concern is keeping your job for another term and trying not to get hurt. That's a hard thing to do in a place like this, isn't it? I'd imagine your best chance for staying out of the line of fire would be to stay on everyone's good side and make yourself scarce when the shooting starts."

The sheriff leveled his eyes on Clint in an attempt to give a hard look. "I'm an honest man, Mister Adams."

"I'm sure you are. But you know what? You're also scared," Clint said, knowing that those other men as well as a good part of the saloon were listening to him. "And while that's as human as the next person, no town can afford to have a scared lawman protecting it. But that's none of my concern, either. It *is* this town's first concern."

Reaching out with a hand that moved so fast, the lawman didn't even have a chance to react to it, Clint snatched the badge pinned to the lawman's shirt pocket and tore it off. He then got to his feet, set the badge down on the middle of the table and said, "The town's second concern should be finding a new sheriff."

The lawman had both hands on the table and was staring about as though he couldn't get himself to believe what had just happened. He started to say something a couple times, but only managed to get out a nonsensical mumble.

Clint tipped his hat to the fellow, downed the rest of his beer and walked away. When he got to the bar, he set some money down and started to head for the door.

"Hey," came a voice from nearby.

Turning to look, Clint found Dave standing there with the coins Clint had just thrown down. "You forgot something."

"That's for the drinks, Dave. Keep the change."

With a smirk and a shake of his head, Dave flipped the

money through the air and into Clint's waiting hand. "Whenever you're in here, paying for your drinks is something else that's none of your concern."

Clint returned the smile and pocketed the money. "Much obliged. I'll check in with you next time I'm in the area."

"You be sure to do that, Mister Adams. Something tells me there's gonna be some changes in this town when you pass through here again."

"Good. And Dave . . . sorry about what happened."

The barkeep's eyes flicked toward the spot on the floor that was still tainted by Jerry's blood. A sad look passed over his face, which showed through the casual façade he'd been holding up this entire time. "Thanks, Mister Adams." Then, looking Clint directly in the eyes, he added, "Thanks for everything."

The Yellow Dog Saloon quieted down for a moment as Clint turned and walked out through the front door. Except for the sheriff, everyone inside the place seemed more than a little sad to watch him go.

A couple moments after he stepped outside, Clint heard all of the saloon's noises come flooding back to life. The voices rose in their excited chatter and the commotion got so thick that it was hard to hear the wind as it whipped down the street.

Shaking his head, Clint knew that of all the things that would change in the town of Clark, the Yellow Dog wouldn't be one of them.

FORTY-TWO

Eager to be on his way and leave the town of Clark to its own problems, Clint headed straight for the livery so he could pick up Eclipse and head out. By the looks of things, it was going to be a dreary day that would more than likely become downright cold before the sun went down. A thick bank of clouds was streaked across the entire sky, blotting out much of the light.

There wasn't much of a wind, but what little breeze there was nipped at any bit of exposed skin it could find, chilling Clint's ears and hands like hundreds of tiny, frozen needles. Even with all of this, Clint was looking forward to getting in a good day's ride and spending the night in front of a roaring campfire. All he needed to do was saddle up the Darley Arabian stallion and do his best to forget about the mess he'd been pulled into over the last couple of days.

As he was thinking this, Clint noticed someone standing on the side of the street. The way she stood and the way she followed him with her eyes told Clint that she was waiting for him to get closer. And when he got a better look at her face, Clint figured he knew why she might be waiting.

"Hello, Abby," Clint said as he came to a stop in front of the brunette.

Although it hadn't been more than an hour since he'd seen her last, Clint noticed a distinct difference about her. She seemed to carry herself with a quieter kind of strength as opposed to the brash, outgoing manner with which she usually carried herself.

Abby's hands were folded in front of her and she smiled in a way that made up for all the coldness in the air. "You're leaving, then?" she asked.

"I think it's about time."

"That's funny . . . because I was thinking the same thing."

Clint was genuinely surprised to hear that and it showed in his face.

Abby must have noticed this as well, because she laughed a little and nodded. "After all that happened, I think I've about had my fill of gunfighters and bad men for a while. Actually . . . for a long while."

"I guess I'm to blame for that," Clint said.

"You certainly are, Clint Adams. But it's not because you're either of those things." Stepping in a little closer, Abby closed her hands behind Clint's neck, pulled him down a bit and kissed him on the lips. It was a short, sweet kiss, but it affected them both just as much as the ones they'd shared in her room. "You've helped me see a few things that I've been missing. And since I've been able to put away a good bit of money, I think I'll go look for those things someplace where I can get a fresh start. Maybe Kansas or California."

"California, huh? You socked away that much?"

"Well, if bad men were good for something besides some excitement, they were always more than willing to part with their earnings."

Rather than ask too many questions about where those earnings had come from, Clint kissed her again and said,

"Good luck to you. I hope you find whatever you're looking for."

"Me too."

And just as she had started to walk away, Abby looked
down the street and then back to Clint. "Looks like I'm
not the only one who wants to say good-bye."

Clint looked in the direction where Abby was pointing
and saw someone standing in front of the livery. He recognized both of their faces and wasn't surprised to see
either of them. He was, however, surprised to see both of
them together.

When he turned back toward Abby, he found that the
brunette had already walked away. She gave him a last
backward glance along with a wave and then set off down
her own path.

From there, Clint took a deep breath and kept walking
toward the stable. Now, more than ever, he just wanted
to get the hell out of this town and be on his way. But as
much as he wanted to do that, it seemed he couldn't escape without wrapping up the last of the business that had
been started here.

Unlike his last couple of words with Abby, this conversation was one that Clint was most definitely not an-
ticipating. It was like pulling an arrow from a wound or
shooting a rabid dog through the head. He didn't want to
do it, but it had to be done and putting it off would only
cause more damage in the long run.

Clint walked toward the livery with quiet confidence.
His eyes locked on the two figures that were standing one
in front of the other, and steeled himself for whatever was
about to happen.

The figure in front was the blonde waitress, Sandra.

Standing behind her was Tom Bolander.

They seemed to be talking intently about something and

the moment he saw Clint coming, Tom drew his pistol and pointed it at Sandra's head.

"All right," Clint thought as his own hand drifted toward the Colt at his side. "Let's get this over with."

FORTY-THREE

Tom grabbed Sandra around the throat with one hand, pulling her so that she was between himself and Clint. The .44 was steady in his hand and he glared at Clint with a newfound intensity. "Not another step, Adams. Or I swear to God I'll blow her brains out."

Taking in the scene without doing anything that might provoke the younger man, Clint stopped where he was and kept his hand within easy reach of his Colt. "I knew I wouldn't have to go looking for you," he said. "Just like I knew you wouldn't take any of the chances I gave you to get away from that spineless weasel you called a teacher."

"This don't have to go no further," Tom said in a rush. "We can just walk away from this and nobody needs to get hurt."

Clint's eyes drilled directly into Tom's, burrowing farther and farther until Clint got a good look at what was happening within the kid's brain. It wasn't anything out of the ordinary that allowed Clint to do such a thing. All he had was his own experience and some natural ability at reading people like ink on a page.

In the end, that was all Clint needed.

"If I wanted to hurt you, kid, you wouldn't have made it out of the Yellow Dog last night. And as for walking away from this . . . you lost your last chance for that when you shot that bartender." Glancing to Sandra, he asked, "Are you all right?"

She nodded weakly, her cheek brushing up against the end of the .44's barrel. Her eyes looked more concerned than frightened. And though she was struggling within the grip Tom was holding her, Sandra wasn't trying too hard to get away.

Clint took a slow step forward, followed by another . . . and then another.

"What're you doing?" Tom asked, his hand shaking. "I said stop where you are!"

"I want you to think, kid. Think about all the times we've gone against each other. Now think about all the times I could have put lead through you easier than picking a bottle off a fencepost."

Clint could tell his words were sinking deeply into Tom's mind. Although the kid tried to keep up the tough exterior, he couldn't keep the nervousness from showing at the corner of his eyes.

"I just want to get out of here," Tom said.

"And that's exactly what you should do," Clint replied in all earnestness. "Get out of here. But since you seem so willing to learn from gunmen, let me give you this one lesson. There's always someone better than you out there. And if you keep testing yourself, you'll only find that out that much quicker."

Narrowing his eyes, Clint added, "And if you keep pulling shit like this, I'll find you myself and we can test those skills of yours for real."

Tom went back and forth between so many different thoughts that he developed a nervous tic not too much different from Niestrom's. He went from tightening his grip on his gun and then on Sandra. All the while, his eyes were locked on Clint until he finally started to take a look over his shoulder.

Whatever it had been that he'd hoped to see, apparently Tom couldn't find it. Looking back to Clint, all of the indecision had drained from his eyes to be replaced by simple resignation. All of the tension had disappeared, taking the tic along with it. His expression was cold and sure.

Third Eye Niestrom would have been proud.

"All right, Gunsmith," Tom said as he shoved Sandra away with enough force to knock her off her balance. "You want to do this right now, then let's go ahead and do it."

Clint watched as Sandra climbed back to her feet and backed herself up against the livery door. She could have run in just about any direction, but she chose to stay right where she was.

A fleeting thought went through Clint's mind that she might be just like the others in this town. The possibility of seeing a real gunfight up-close and personal might have been enough to keep her from fleeing for safer ground, but somehow Clint didn't believe it. He knew there was something else going on with her, but now was simply not the time to deal with it.

He had another more pressing matter to tend to and a lesson that needed to be taught.

Tom had been holding the .44 in his right hand when all he needed to do was use it to threaten a woman. Now that he had to defend his own life, he felt the pain in that hand even more intensely than when Clint had first put a bullet through it. His fingers wriggled against the grip like four worms and sweat began to form on his palms.

"Tell you what," Clint said as he took notice of the kid's predicament. "I'll make this fair. If you want to switch hands, then so will I." And without waiting for Tom's response, Clint loosened his gun belt just enough to create some slack and then wedged his right hand through the leather strap all the way down past the wrist.

Once he was sufficiently restrained, Clint flexed the fingers on his left hand and said, "There. Now we're both lefties. Is that fair enough for you?"

Taking his time while watching Clint suspiciously, Tom handed the .44 over from his wounded right hand and into his left. He held the pistol down at his side while adjusting his fingers around its grip. When he was certain that Clint wasn't about to trick him, some of Tom's confidence began to show on his face.

Tom kept his eyes firmly locked on to Clint, watching every little move that his opponent was making. Just as he'd been taught, Tom noticed the way Clint shifted once on his feet and the way he pulled in his breaths. Finally, Tom saw what he'd been waiting for as Clint stretched out his left arm as if trying to work a kink out.

In one motion, Tom brought up his pistol. Before it was on target, he heard a subtle brushing sound that reminded him of someone slipping into a coat. And with that sound still going through his ears, Tom realized that he was staring straight down into the barrel of Clint's gun.

He hadn't even seen Clint's arm move across his body, although it would have had to do just that in order to draw the weapon.

Clint's eyes were colder than the iron in his hand. "Now let's see if you've learned your lesson," he said.

Still holding the .44 with his thumb resting on the uncocked hammer, Tom let out the breath he'd been holding and lowered his eyes. He relaxed his fingers and let the pistol drop heavily to the dirt.

Stepping forward so he could kick Tom's pistol away, Clint flipped his Colt back into his right hand and dropped it into his holster. "Class dismissed."

FORTY-FOUR

Two nights later, Clint sat on his folded bedroll and prodded a stick into the heart of a roaring campfire. With the town of Clark well behind him, he thought back to what had happened and couldn't help but breathe a long, loud sigh.

"Something wrong?" came a voice from beside him.

Clint looked over at the only reason this moment was better than he'd thought it could have been. Abby stared back at him with a warm smile, which was made even warmer by the flickering glow of the flames in front of her.

"Nothing's wrong," he said. "Just relieved."

"Relieved that you're back on the trail, or because I decided to come with you as far as the next train station?"

"Both."

Abby turned to look into the fire. As she did, her lips curled into a sly grin and she started to laugh quietly.

"Should I ask?" Clint said. "Or do I even want to know?"

"I was thinking about what you said to the sheriff. When Dave told me about it, he damn near burst out laughing and the sheriff was still sitting no more than ten feet away."

Clint shook his head and kept prodding the fire, making sure that the pieces of wood burned evenly.

"Do you think he'll take care of Tom?"

"The sheriff might be frightened and lazy, but even he should be able to handle a killer that gets hand-delivered into his jail. If not, then the kid deserves to get away."

"Do you really think that?"

After a slight pause, Clint shook his head. "No. He'll probably hang. And the fact of the matter is that he deserves that too."

"Then why didn't you just shoot him?" Abby asked. "If he was going to wind up dead, why go through all the trouble you did when it could've been over so much quicker?"

"Because that's what he wanted. If he couldn't be known for killing me, he would be known for going up against me. At least . . . that's what he'd be known for once all those gossips at the Yellow Dog got done telling the story. This way, he's just some killer who got what he deserved at the end of a noose. Just like so many other bad men that came before him."

Shifting so that she was facing him rather than the fire, Abby scooted in closer to Clint and then climbed onto his lap. "So what about Sandra?" she asked. "Wasn't she waiting for you by the livery also?"

"Yes she was. I never got much of a chance to say anything to her. Once Tom gave himself up, she made herself scarce."

"Well that's good, because if she didn't, I would have had to get rid of her myself."

Abby slipped her hands beneath Clint's jacket and started pulling apart the buttons on his shirt. Her fingers slid against his chest and she whispered into his ear. "You don't have to think about any of that anymore. It's all over and that just leaves you . . . and me."

Clint's hands were busy as well. Despite the chill in the air, the skin of Abby's thigh felt warm beneath her skirt. Her body was even warmer as he followed the curve of her leg all the way up and cupped her bottom. "Thank god for that," he said before moving her onto the ground and settling on top of her.

FORTY-FIVE

The deputy showed her in through the sheriff's office and led her all the way toward the back of the building. That was where the row of three cells were built, only one of which was currently occupied.

"You sure you want to be here alone?" the youthful deputy asked.

Sandra nodded solemnly. "Yes. I'll be fine."

The deputy shot a mean glare down toward the prisoner and walked back toward the office.

Inside the cell, Tom accepted the other man's threatening gaze in stride. After the last couple of days, the deputy's attempt to scare him almost seemed comical in comparison. Once the deputy had gone, Tom looked through the bars at the blonde and said, "I knew you wouldn't let me down. Do you remember what we talked about?"

Sandra thought back to when it had been just her and Tom in front of the livery. Although Clint Adams had interrupted things, that had only made the entire day that much more exciting in her mind. "I remember," she said. "What kind of ace in the hole would I be if I didn't remember?"

Getting up from the narrow wooden cot that was the cell's only furnishing, he stepped up to the bars and wrapped his hands around the cold steel.

Watching him was enough to send a hot wave through her flesh. She thought about all the things Tom had done and all the things he'd said. He'd even stood up to the Gunsmith, which made him all the more appealing to her. Sandra paused for a second to gather her strength. Once she did, she stood up straight and fixed her eyes hungrily upon him.

Tom studied the blonde for a moment, sizing her up just the way Niestrom had taught him. Just to be sure, he reached through the bars and put his hand on Sandra's waist. Smiling lewdly, he moved his hand up until he could cup one of her full, round breasts.

Sure enough, the woman pulled in a quick breath and didn't move away. She wanted him.

"I don't have much time," he said.

"If I do this, I want to come with you."

Tom nodded. "I'll give you the ride of your life," he promised while his eyes moved up and down her body. "But I can't do that from in here."

Bending at the waist, Sandra pulled up the bottom of her skirt to reveal a shapely leg encased in a sheer black stocking. Tucked in the material, right next to where the garter belt hooked in place, there was a two-shot Derringer. She removed the pistol and kept her skirt hiked up for another second until she knew Tom was staring anxiously at her revealed flesh.

"The sheriff's not here," she whispered while slipping the Derringer into Tom's hand.

"Just the one in that office?"

Sandra nodded.

Tom held the Derringer so that it was mostly hidden behind one arm. He thumbed back the hammer and positioned himself so that he could hit anything in the hall-way . . . even with his left hand.

Sandra stood so Tom could hide behind her and got ready to jump aside. She could already feel the excitement her new life would bring. And it all started right now. "Deputy," she called out, "could you come here for a moment?"

Watch for

TANGLED WEB

253rd novel in the exciting GUNSMITH series
from Jove

Coming in January!

J. R. ROBERTS
THE GUNSMITH

THE GUNSMITH #241:	PLAYING FOR BLOOD	0-515-13231-4
THE GUNSMITH #242:	DEAD AND BURIED	0-515-13253-5
THE GUNSMITH #243:	OUTLAW LUCK	0-515-13267-5
THE GUNSMITH #244:	THE SHADOW OF THE GUNSMITH	0-515-13282-9
THE GUNSMITH #245:	GHOST SQUADRON	0-515-13297-7
THE GUNSMITH #246:	DEAD MAN'S EYES	0-515-13312-4
THE GUNSMITH #247:	RANDOM GUNFIRE	0-515-13338-8
THE GUNSMITH #248:	A MAN OF THE GUN	0-515-13352-3
THE GUNSMITH #249:	DEADLY GAME	0-515-13369-8
THE GUNSMITH #250:	THE DOOMSDAY RIDERS	0-515-13391-4
THE GUNSMITH #251:	NEXT TO DIE	0-515-13407-4

Delivers more bang for the buck!

Available wherever books are sold or
to order call:
1-800-788-6262

(Ad # B11B)

LONGARM

**Explore the exciting Old West with one
of the men who made it wild!**

JAKE LOGAN
TODAY'S HOTTEST ACTION WESTERN!